Erle Stanley Gardner and The Murder Room

>>> This title is part of The Murder Room, our series dedicated to making available out-of-print or hard-to-find titles by classic crime writers.

Crime fiction has always held up a mirror to society. The Victorians were fascinated by sensational murder and the emerging science of detection; now we are obsessed with the forensic detail of violent death. And no other genre has so captivated and enthralled readers.

Vast troves of classic crime writing have for a long time been unavailable to all but the most dedicated frequenters of second-hand bookshops. The advent of digital publishing means that we are now able to bring you the backlists of a huge range of titles by classic and contemporary crime writers, some of which have been out of print for decades.

From the genteel amateur private eyes of the Golden Age and the femmes fatales of pulp fiction, to the morally ambiguous hard-boiled detectives of mid twentieth-century America and their descendants who walk our twenty-first century streets, The Murder Room has it all. >>>

The Murder Room
Where Criminal Minds Meet

themurderroom.com

Erle Stanley Gardner (1889–1970)

Born in Malden, Massachusetts, Erle Stanley Gardner left school in 1909 and attended Valparaiso University School of Law in Indiana for just one month before he was suspended for focusing more on his hobby of boxing that his academic studies. Soon after, he settled in California, where he taught himself the law and passed the state bar exam in 1911. The practise of law never held much interest for him, however, apart from as it pertained to trial strategy, and in his spare time he began to write for the pulp magazines that gave Dashiell Hammett and Raymond Chandler their start. Not long after the publication of his first novel, *The Case of the Velvet Claws*, featuring Perry Mason, he gave up his legal practice to write full time. He had one daughter, Grace, with his first wife, Natalie, from whom he later separated. In 1968 Gardner married his long-term secretary, Agnes Jean Bethell, whom he professed to be the real 'Della Street', Perry Mason's sole (although unacknowledged) love interest. He was one of the most successful authors of all time and at the time of his death, in Temecula, California in 1970, is said to have had 135 million copies of his books in print in America alone.

By Erle Stanley Gardner
(titles below include only those
published in the Murder Room)

Perry Mason series

The Case of the Sulky Girl
(1933)
The Case of the Baited Hook
(1940)
The Case of the Borrowed
Brunette (1946)
The Case of the Lonely
Heiress (1948)
The Case of the Negligent
Nymph (1950)
The Case of the Moth-Eaten
Mink (1952)
The Case of the Glamorous
Ghost (1955)
The Case of the Terrified
Typist (1956)
The Case of the Gilded Lily
(1956)
The Case of the Lucky Loser
(1957)
The Case of the Long-Legged
Models (1958)
The Case of the Deadly Toy
(1959)
The Case of the Singing Skirt
(1959)

The Case of the Duplicate
Daughter (1960)
The Case of the Blonde
Bonanza (1962)

Cool and Lam series
*First published under the
pseudonym A.A. Fair*

The Bigger They Come (1939)
Turn on the Heat (1940)
Gold Comes in Bricks (1940)
Spill the Jackpot (1941)
Double or Quits (1941)
Owls Don't Blink (1942)
Bats Fly at Dusk (1942)
Cats Prowl at Night (1943)
Crows Can't Count (1946)
Fools Die on Friday (1947)
Bedrooms Have Windows
(1949)
Some Women Won't Wait (1953)
Beware the Curves (1956)
You Can Die Laughing (1957)
Some Slips Don't Show (1957)
The Count of Nine (1958)
Pass the Gravy (1959)
Kept Women Can't Quit (1960)

Bachelors Get Lonely (1961)
Shills Can't Count Chips (1961)
Try Anything Once (1962)
Fish or Cut Bait (1963)
Up For Grabs (1964)
Cut Thin to Win (1965)
Widows Wear Weeds (1966)
Traps Need Fresh Bait (1967)

Doug Selby D.A. series

The D.A. Calls it Murder (1937)
The D.A. Holds a Candle (1938)
The D.A. Draws a Circle (1939)
The D.A. Goes to Trial (1940)
The D.A. Cooks a Goose (1942)
The D.A. Calls a Turn (1944)

The D.A. Takes a Chance (1946)
The D.A. Breaks an Egg (1949)

Terry Clane series

Murder Up My Sleeve (1937)
The Case of the Backward
   Mule (1946)

Gramp Wiggins series

The Case of the Turning Tide
   (1941)
The Case of the Smoking
   Chimney (1943)

Two Clues (two novellas) (1947)

Cut Thin to Win

Erle Stanley Gardner

An Orion book

Copyright © The Erle Stanley Gardner Trust 1965

This edition published by
The Orion Publishing Group Ltd
Orion House
5 Upper St Martin's Lane
London WC2H 9EA

An Hachette UK company
A CIP catalogue record for this book is available from the British Library

ISBN 978 1 4719 0922 1

www.orionbooks.co.uk

CHAPTER ONE

The sign on the frosted glass of the door read:

B. COOL
and
DONALD LAM
PRIVATE INVESTIGATORS
Hours: 9 – 5
Entrance

I opened the door, walked in, nodded to the receptionist and crossed over to the door marked: DONALD LAM, *Private*.

Elsie Brand, my secretary, said, "Did you notice the man who's waiting in the outer office?"

"Not particularly. Why?"

"He wants to see you."

"What about?"

"Something that is so highly confidential he won't discuss it with anyone except you."

"What's his name?"

She handed me a card. The ink embossing had been piled on so thick a blind man could have read it with the tips of his fingers.

The card read, DAWSON RE-DEBENTURE DISCOUNT SECURITY COMPANY. Down in the left hand corner were the words, *Clayton Dawson, Assistant to the President*.

The address of the company was Denver, Colorado.

"All right," I said to Elsie, "let's see him."

Elsie buzzed the receptionist and said, "Mr. Lam is in now. Have Mr. Dawson come in."

A few moments later the receptionist opened the door for Dawson.

He was medium height, around fifty, wearing clothes that were quiet and subdued in pattern but of a quality which made them stand out. There was a rich luster about the cloth.

He looked around the office and let his eyes focus on me the second time around.

"Mr. Lam?"

There was just a touch of incredulity in his voice.

"Yes," I said.

He didn't sit down. He looked at Elsie Brand; then he looked at me, then he shook his head and said, "I'm sorry, I don't want to hurt your feelings, but it's better to do it now than later. I'm afraid you just won't do."

"Get someone who will do then."

"I had expected a much bigger man."

"You want an investigator?"

"Yes."

"What did you want him to do, play pro football or investigate?"

"I . . . well, I understand that in your profession you have to face certain odds, odds which sometimes require a degree of physical proficiency.

"I have no doubt that you're very skillful and highly competent but, for the type of job I have in mind—What about your partner?

"Is Mr. Cool more . . . more beefy?"

I said, "For your information, B. Cool *is* a bit more beefy."

His face lit up.

"The 'B'," I said, "stands for 'Bertha.' B. Cool is a woman."

Dawson sat down suddenly, as though his knees had given away. "Oh, my God!" he said.

I said, "You've probably been reading novels where the private investigator is trapped in a washroom with two torpedoes bearing down on him with knives. He grabs the wrist of the first torpedo, twists the knife out of his hand with such a jerk that it flies to the ceiling and sticks there. At the same time, he kicks the other assailant in the stomach.

"Then crashing his knuckles into the face of the first man, he can feel the crunching of bone as a nose flattens under the blow, and has the satisfaction of seeing blood spatter like drops from the nozzle of a garden hose.

"The man staggers backward for two steps, then crashes through a swinging door and comes to a sitting position.

"That gives our hero an idea. He lifts the other unconscious man from the floor and seats him in another stall.

"The door swings shut. The detective washes his hands under the warm water faucet and is drying them under an air dryer when the door of the rest room bursts open and two police come in and stare about them as our hero pauses in front of the mirror to adjust his tie.

2

" 'Any trouble in here?' one of the cops asks.

"Our hero raises his eyebrows in surprise. 'Trouble?' he askes. 'Not for me—' "

"You don't need to go on," Dawson said.

"I can," I told him. "Indefinitely."

"You've evidently been reading that stuff yourself."

"Why not? If you can put yourself in the position of the hero, it's fun to live in that sort of a world."

"But you couldn't do it in reality," he said.

"Neither could you," I told him. "Bertha Cool is the only one I know who might."

He looked me over thoughtfully. "The deuce of it is your firm has one hell of a reputation. I personally know of two very difficult jobs you've handled."

"Muscle jobs?" I asked.

He hesitated, then said, "Brain jobs, I guess. What sort of a woman is this Mrs. Cool?"

"You'd better look her over," I said.

"There's a woman involved in this case," he told me.

"There usually is."

" It might be . . . it just *might* be that, in a matter of this kind, your Bertha Cool could do a job."

"I don't see why not."

"The girl is young, wayward, obstinate, independent, impudent and ungrateful."

"In other words," I said, "she's a thoroughly normal, modern young woman. Is she, by any chance, your sweetheart, or rather, was she before the serpent entered the Garden of Eden?"

He said with dignity, "She is my daughter."

"I see," I told him. "Perhaps you'd like to talk with Mrs. Cool?"

"I think it would be advantageous to have her in on the conversation."

I nodded to Elsie Brand.

Elsie put through a call on Bertha Cool's line and, a moment later, I heard the rasping sound of Bertha Cool's voice.

Elsie explained the situation briefly.

She hung up the phone and said, "Mrs. Cool will be right in."

A few moments later the door opened, and Bertha Cool entered the room.

Bertha was built like an old-fashioned freight locomotive. She had short legs, a big torso, diamond-hard glittering eyes, and as she came barging into the office it was quite evident that she wasn't in her most amiable mood. She always liked to rely on the prerogative of her sixty-odd years and be the senior partner. She would have preferred to have Dawson brought in to her office with a proper fanfare.

"Mrs. Cool," I said with my best company manners, "may I present Mr. Dawson, assistant to the president of the Dawson Re-Debenture Discount Security Company."

Dawson jumped to his feet.

Bertha's glittering eyes looked him over. "How do you do, Mister Dawson," she said.

Dawson bowed. "It is a distinct pleasure, an honor," he declared.

Bertha Cool turned to me. "Business or social?"

"Business," I told her. "Mr. Dawson wants to talk with us about a case. He feels there may be some trouble connected with it which I can't handle."

"What sort of trouble?" Bertha asked.

"Violence," I said.

"No, just a minute, just a minute," Dawson interposed. "I didn't exactly say it in that way."

"You intimated it," I countered.

He started explaining to Bertha. "I merely suggested," he said, "that is was my understanding that private investigators had to be a little broader, a little heavier and a little older than your partner; that, at times, they encountered violence."

"We get by," Bertha said.

"I daresay you do."

"There's a woman in the deal," I said to Bertha, "and Mr. Dawson thought that might complicate the situation somewhat."

"It always complicates any situation," Bertha said.

She heaved herself into a chair. Diamonds scintillated as she moved her hands. She saw to it that they did. Her eyes glittered as she surveyed Dawson.

"Want to tell us about it?" she asked.

"It is," he said, "a matter which will involve the utmost delicacy of approach."

"We've never had one that didn't," Bertha told him.

"It's a family matter."

I handed Bertha the embossed card.

Bertha rubbed a speculative thumbnail over the embossing, said abruptly to Dawson, "You're assistant to the president?"

"That's right."

"Your name's Dawson?"

"Yes. Clayton Dawson."

"But the name is the Dawson Re-Debenture Discount Security Company. How come you have the same name?"

He said, "It was founded by my father."

"Your father's no longer alive?"

"He's retired. He's chairman of the board."

"Then how come you're not the president?"

"I see no reason to discuss my personal family affairs, Mrs. Cool," Dawson said with dignity, "but it happens that my older brother is president."

"I see," Bertha said. "All right, what's the pitch?"

"I beg your pardon?"

"What's this all about? What do you want us to do?"

Dawson looked from Bertha to me, then looked back to Bertha.

"I have a daughter," he said.

Bertha sat silent.

"She is twenty-three. She is undisciplined, ungrateful, and I am afraid, if judged by strictly old-fashioned standards, immoral."

"People don't judge women by strictly old-fashioned standards these days," Bertha said. "They've gone out of style. What's the specific problem?"

"When it became apparent that she was not going to be amenable to discipline and seemed intent on disgracing the family name, I terminated all financial contributions. In other words, I made it plain to her that if she was going to ignore my wishes and no longer consider me as her mentor, I would no longer be financially responsible in any way."

"And what did she do?"

"She walked out."

"This scene took place in Denver, Colorado?" I asked.

His eyes shifted to me, looked down at his feet for a moment, then raised back to mine.

"Yes."

"Go on," I told him.

"My daughter," he said, "left home. She came to Los Angeles. She got all tangled up with a man. I do not approve of the alliance; I do not approve of the man."

"You've met him?"

"Yes."

"What's his name?"

"Sidney Eldon."

"What's your daughter's name?"

"Phyllis. P-h-y-l-l-i-s."

"You seem to have kept up with your daughter."

"She has written me occasionally."

"How long since she left?"

"About two months."

"Why do you come to us?"

He fidgeted around slightly, shifting his position two or three times in the chair.

"Quit stalling," I told him. "Something is bringing all this to a head. What's your problem?"

He said, "I don't know whether you people can help me."

"Neither do I," I told him.

He glanced at me sharply.

Bertha said, "What Donald means is that hiring a firm of private investigators makes rather an expensive way to solve a romantic problem."

"Money," Dawson said, snapping his fingers, "is nothing."

Bertha's face softened. "I see," she cooed. "It's a matter of principle with you."

"Exactly," he said. "That and the family name."

"What about the family name?" I asked.

He said, "Anything that I tell you is confidential?"

"Yes."

"As private detectives, are you licensed?"

"Yes."

"If you should cover up evidence of a crime, you would lose that license?"

"That's right."

"Therefore, you can't take employment which would cause you to lose your license."

"You're doing the talking," I said, as Bertha hesitated.

"Therefore," he said, "if I should be *entirely* frank with you, you couldn't accept the employment and you couldn't protect me, and on the other hand, if you are going to protect me in the way I want, I can't be *entirely* frank with you."

"Deals of that sort," I warned, "are apt to run into a hell of a lot of money."

Bertha beamed at me.

Dawson bent down, opened his brief case and took out an envelope. From the envelope he extracted a small, torn fragment of cloth. He handed the torn fragment of cloth to Bertha.

Bertha's diamonds glittered as she turned the cloth over in her fingers. "What's this?" she asked.

"I have to express this very carefully so that I will not put you in a precarious position and so I will not put myself in a dangerous position," Dawson said. "It is possible someone might claim that piece of cloth *could* have been found adhering to an automobile which my daughter was falsely accused of driving on the fifth of this month, at a time when she was more or less under the influence of liquor."

Bertha said, "You mean that—"

"Shut up. Bertha," I said.

Bertha glowered at me.

I said, "Dawson has expressed himself in unmistakable language. This situation requires very careful consideration and we mustn't say anything which would put our client in a precarious position."

Dawson nodded emphatically.

The idea began to soak into Bertha's mind. She let her eyes shift from one to the other of us.

"We can't cut corners, Donald," she warned.

"Certainly not," I told her. "So far, no one has shown us any corners which could be cut. I take it, Mr. Dawson, that you're not prepared to tell us who discovered this piece of cloth or what significance it has?"

Dawson said piously, "I don't know that it has *any* significance. That is why I am coming to you. I would like to have you find out what significance, if any, that cloth does have."

"And if it should have some significance, what do you want to do?"

"Take it from there in the best way possible," he said.

"You have regard for your family's good name but no particular affection for your daughter, is that right?" Bertha asked.

"That is not right. I love my daughter very much but I have worn out my patience. I am now afraid she has placed me in such a position that I cannot show my love . . . at least, openly. Anything that is done would have to be done under cover and behind the scenes, so to speak, very much under cover."

"Your daughter's living here?"

"Yes."

"As Phyllis Dawson?"

"No, as Phyllis Eldon. She is living with this man, Sidney Eldon."

"Where?"

"The Parkridge Apartments."

"What does Sidney Eldon do? How does he get by?"

"I am afraid he is, at least at present, getting by on my daughter's money."

"She has some money?"

"She took some money with her, when she left—and I don't want you trying to check on that in any way because, if you did, it would attract attention, and right at the moment I don't want to attract attention."

"Just what do you want?" I asked.

"I want matters handled swiftly, efficiently and quietly. If that fragment of cloth has any significance, I want the situation handled so there are no embarrassing repercussions."

"Put the cloth back in your brief case," I told him.

"But I wanted you to see it."

"We've seen it."

"But you may need it so you can be sure—"

"We don't want to be sure," I told him. "If we're going to help you, or help your daughter, we can't afford to be sure of anything. You should understand the implications."

Slowly, he put the cloth back in the envelope, the envelope back in the brief case.

"Now then," I said, "if you want us to represent you, we don't want to know anything more. We'll get the facts from our own investigation. You want to find out what you daughter's been doing, is that right?"

"That's right."

"You don't *know*?"

"No, I suspect that she's—"

"We don't want suspicions," I broke in. "All we want to know is that you want us to find out about your daughter. We'll investigate in our own way."

"I see," he said. There was a note of relief in his voice.

"That," Bertha said swiftly, "is going to cost you a hundred dollars a day and expenses with no guarantee on results."

"Plus a retainer," I added quickly, "of five hundred dollars, payable in advance."

"As I told you," he said "money is no object."

Bertha said, "Now, if it should appear that—"

"I think your partner understands the situation, Mrs. Cool," Dawson interposed quickly.

Dawson turned to me. "I beg your pardon for doubting your competency, Mr. Lam. You have a very quick alert mind."

He took a billfold from his pocket, took out a stack of one-hundred dollar bills. "Here," he said, "is a retainer of five hundred dollars, three hundred dollars for expenses, and pay in advance for seven days of investigative work. When the matter is concluded you can send me a telegram, care of the company in Denver, Colorado, or write me a letter. Be sure to mark either the letter or the telegram personal."

"I'll have the bookkeeper make a receipt," Bertha Cool said.

"Good heavens, no," Dawson exclaimed. He once more turned to me. "I think you understand the situation, Mr. Lam."

He shot his left arm out so that he could look at his wristwatch, made clucking noises with his tongue against the roof of his mouth, said, "I am running farther behind schedule than I thought. I must leave. Goodbye."

He virtually ran out of the office.

Bertha turned to me and said, "Well, you were so goddam smart, I hope you know what it is all about."

"I think I do," I said.

"Well, I'm your partner," she reminded me.

"I think our friend, Mr. Clayton Dawson, is in a jam," I said, "and he expects us to get him out."

"*He's* in a jam?" Bertha asked.

"Yes."

"He said it was his daughter."

"I heard what he said."

"You don't think that it is his daughter?" she asked, puzzled.

"Let's put it this way," I said, "I don't think she *is* his daughter."

"Then who is she?"

"His witness."

"But she's Eldon's mistress."

"So he said."

"Then who the devil is this Sidney Eldon?" Bertha asked.

"He could be our client," I said. "Clayton Dawson to you."

Bertha jumped as though her chair had been wired. "We can't take on a case of that sort," she said.

"What sort?"

"The kind your intimating."

"I haven't intimated anything about the *case*," I said, "only about the *client*."

Bertha shook her head.

I said to Elsie, "Take this money out to the bookkeeper. Tell her to deposit it and credit Clayton Dawson of Denver."

Bertha's greedy eyes focused on the pile of money. "Fry me

for an oyster," she said. She heaved herself up out of the chair. "It's your baby," she announced, "and you can change the diapers."

She waddled out of the office.

CHAPTER TWO

Automobile injury cases, these days, are a dime a dozen. They are seldom worthy of a separate place in the news. They are lumped together.

John Doe gets killed in an intersection. It isn't even worthy of a separate news item. Joe Doakes, driving home at three o'clock in the morning, "loses control" of his car and wraps it around a telephone pole. Joe is killed and Jane Whosis, a female companion, aged twenty-three, of 7918 Whatsis Street, is seriously injured.

A station wagon jumps over the dividing line on the freeway, careers out of control in the wrong lane, smacks another car head on, kills two people, scatters children all over the freeway, and some newspaper rewrite man bundles up the whole list of accidents, gives them one headline; then in four or five short paragraphs, disposes of the whole business.

The accident I thought I wanted was buried in a newspaper five days earlier. A Mrs. Harvey W. Chester had been in a pedestrian crossing. She was struck down, the victim of a hit-and-run driver.

The police learned that a small piece had been torn from the skirt she was wearing, so they felt that identification of the car and apprehension of the driver would be only a matter of time, inasmuch as there was one other clue which the police were not disclosing.

Mrs. Harvey W. Chester was forty-eight years old and resided at 2367-A Doorman Avenue. Her injuries were listed as "serious."

The account then went on to describe a head-on collison and the apprehension of a stolen car, after a chase which at times reached the speed of one hundred and five miles an hour.

When the car had finally been forced to a halt, the driver had calmly stepped out and smilingly informed the police that since he was a juvenile they couldn't lay a finger on him.

Such accidents as resulted in smashed automobiles, minor injuries, etc., were not newsworthy enough to be included.

It was all part of the pattern of life in a big city.

I purchased a bunch of magazines at the newsstand, put them

under my arm, got the agency jalopy, and drove out to Doorman Avenue.

I parked the car two blocks away from the house I wanted. I called at three houses and asked each woman who came to the door if she would like to subscribe to magazines.

In all three instances my reception was somewhat less than cordial.

Having established the proper foundation, I went to 2367.

It was one of the deep lots left over from an earlier era of planning and building. The house in front, which was 2367, was a huge, old-fashioned affair, rambling, filled with waste space; a wide cement walk led around to 2367-A, which was a toy-sized bungalow in the back lot.

I climbed a couple of steps to a miniature porch and rang the doorbell.

A woman's voice called out, "Who is it?"

"A man who has something for you," I said.

"Come in," the tired voice said. "You'll have to open the door yourself."

I opened the door and walked in.

A rather slender woman with high cheekbones and tired eyes was propped up in a wheelchair with her right ankle and her right forearm in bandages; a blanket was folded across her lap and the left leg. The right leg was protruding out through a fold in the blanket.

"Hello," she said.

"Well, hello," I greeted her. "You look as if you'd been in an accident."

"Hit-and-run," she said.

"That's too bad," I told her, spreading out the magazines.

"What do you want, young man? When I told you to come in. I thought you were someone else."

"Who?"

"Just someone else."

"I'm selling magazines," I said. "Subscriptions to magazines."

"I'm not interested."

I said, "You should be, if you don't mind my saying so, because quite apparently you're laid up with nothing much to do."

"I have my radio."

"Don't you get awfully tired of listening to disk jockeys, conversational patter and the same old type of commercial?"

"Yes, I do."

"Subscriptions to these magazines would help you."

"What do you have?"

I handed her six of the magazines that I had picked up.

"These cover a wide field," I said. "They're educational. They tell you things about the house, about the world in general, about the political situation. They're really essential to a person who wants to keep up with the world."

"Tell me some more about them."

She handed me one magazine. "Tell me about the contents of this one."

"That," I said, "is a magazine of general woman's interest. It gives you tips on the home, on menus for high-protein, low-calorie meals. It tells you how to plan a house with the different areas in mind, how to take advantage of a view."

"That's all right," she said. "That's the stuff in this issue of the magazine you have with you, but what are the editors *going* to publish? What's going to come out in the later issues?"

"Articles along the same general line," I said. "The magazine has an established pattern and a reputation to live up to."

"By whom will these articles be written?"

"The outstanding writers on the subject in the country."

"Name one."

"I can't give you the names of the writers who are going to appear. All I can tell you is that it's edited with an up-to-the-minute recognition of the problems of the modern housewife."

"Humph," she said. "What's the next one?"

"That," I said "specialises on homes. It tells you—"

"What's the next issue going to be like?"

"Very similar to this one."

"What's in the Christmas issue?" she asked.

"The editor has gone in for a touching collection of human interest stories that—"

"By whom?" she asked. "Who are the writers?"

"The leading writers in the field."

"Don't you know anything other than that?"

"Well, I feel that that's enough."

"Who are the leading writers in the field?"

"Just look at the table of contents in this magazine," I said, "and you'll get the names."

I started to open the magazine.

"Young man," she said, "you're a liar,"

I stopped and looked up at her.

"They told me about you," she said. "You're the man I was expecting after all."

"Who told you about me?"

"Friends. They said a man representing the insurance company would call on me when I least expected it; that he'd start talking about something else and then lead the subject around to my injuries and try making a settlement."

"I'm not interested in making a settlement," I said. "I'm here to sell magazines."

"Let me see one of your subscription blanks."

"I don't have them with me this morning. I am at present taking orders; then I report them to the office and the follow-up man who does the legwork and the detail work comes down with the actual subscriptions."

"Phooey," she said. "How much?"

"How much for what?"

"For a settlement."

I said, "I'm not representing any insurance company. I'm not representing anyone who is interested in a settlement."

"All right," she said, "never mind whom you're representing. How much?"

I said, "I tell you what I *could* do. I know a friend who sometimes speculates in personal injury cases. He buys up the claims for cash and gets an assignment and then he brings suit. He recovers, of course, a lot more money than he's paid the person who was injured. Everyone has to make a profit."

"Who is this person?" she asked.

"I'm not at liberty to give you his name, but if you're interested in some form of a cash settlement, I might be able to get you in touch with him."

"He'd pay me money and take over my claim and prosecute it and be entitled to everything he got out of it?"

"That's right. It might not be that simple. There's a little trouble with assignment of claims of this nature. You'd probably have to sign an instrument that, for value received, you agreed to turn over to him all of the money that you received as the result of a lawsuit; that he would finance the lawsuit and provide you with an attorney; that he could make any kind of a settlement he wanted; that he could let the matter drop at any time he wanted; that you would be guided by his wishes in the matter; that he would be substituted in your shoes and, in the event of any recovery in your name, you would turn over all the monies to him. In other words, he'd buy you out—lock, stock and barrel."

"For how much?"

"That depends. How serious are you injuries?"

"I hurt all over."

"How many broken bones?"

She said, "I know darned well that bone in my leg is broken, but the doctors tell me it isn't. The X rays don't show it, but I can tell from the way it feels.

"I wouldn't go through this again for thousands of dollars. I can hardly move. I'm so sore."

I said, "Sometimes this man that I know of makes quite a profit on these injuries; and sometimes, after he looks into them, he finds that he's on the losing side of the case and he just backs away and lets the whole thing drop. If he decided to do that in this case, you'd have to sign a release if he told you to."

"But that would be after he'd put up the money?"

"Yes."

"I'd sign," she said.

"Tell me about the facts in the case."

"Well—Look here, young man, you're not fooling me a bit. You're from the insurance company and what you want is a release, but you're trying to make it sound like a speculative investment so you can get it for less money than you would pay otherwise . . . You know all about the facts as much as I do, or maybe more."

I smiled at her and said, "You're rather shrewd and very, very suspicious, Mrs. Chester."

"Do you blame me?"

"No," I said, and then added, "it probably doesn't make any difference. You have a figure in your mind that you'd be willing to accept as a cash settlement. In that way, you'd have the money in cash right now and you could move out of these cramped quarters, go to a nursing home or a hotel where you could get good service and be a lot more comfortable."

"What I'd like to do," she said, "would be to buy a television set with one of those remote control devices so you can turn it on and change stations."

"I am quite satisfied that could be arranged—provided, of course, you didn't want too much."

"You still clinging to this story of yours about knowing somebody that wants to just buy my claim on a speculative basis?"

"That's right. That's the story. That's all anybody would be doing."

"Fifteen thousand dollars," she said.

I smiled and shook my head, then added, "You haven't even told me the facts of the case yet."

"It was hit-and-run," she said. "I was in an intersection mind-ing my own business and this car came swooping around the corner and down the street. Some young woman was driving it. I didn't get a good look at her."

"Do you know the make of the car?"

"No."

I said, "Of course, my man would have to take a chance on being able to find the car."

"That's going to be easy."

"What makes you think so?"

"The police told me that one of the hardest crimes to get away with these days was a hit-and-run; that they have so many scientific gadgets that they're able to spot the car usually within twenty-four hours."

"How long has it been since the accident?"

"Five or six days, almost a week. I haven't figured it up exactly. Let's see, it was—"

"But it's been over forty-eight hours?"

"Certainly. I said it had been—let's see, I believe it's five days. This is the sixth day."

"And the police haven't uncovered anyone yet?" I said. "Every day that passes by without uncovering the culprit makes it that much harder, and makes your claim worth that much less."

Her eyes were shrewd. "Open that closet door, young man, and hand me that dress."

I opened the door, handed her the dress that was just inside.

She spread out the dress, showed me where a small segment had been torn from the cloth. "That piece was ripped out when the car hit me," she said. "Police tell me some fibers from that dress are bound to be clinging to some part of the undercarriage of a car with a dented fender. They'll find it."

The cloth in the dress was the same as the piece Dawson had shown me.

I said, "That may be true, but if they do uncover the driver of the car, it may be that he or she just doesn't have a dime, and no insurance—"

"Phooey," she said, "that was one of those high-class cars—the kind that go like a rocket, and I know this woman had insur-ance because you're here. You're representing the insurance company."

I shook my head.

"All right," she said, "I'll make you a proposition—a take-it-leave-it proposition. If your man wants to give me ten thousand dollars in cold hard cash right now—right this minute—I'll assign my claim."

"Then what would you do?" I asked.

"What would you want me to do?"

I said, "it might be that this man would prefer to make a settlement out of court that no one knew anything about. In that case, he wouldn't want to have the police working too hard on the case."

"I'll get out," she said. "I'll be hard to find. I'll fix it so the police can't trace me; but it has to be ten thousand dollars in cash, and I have to have it within the next twelve hours."

I smiled and shook my head. "That's impossible," I said. "It might take me that long to even locate the man I have in mind and then it might turn out that he isn't interested in a deal of this sort. All I know is that occasionally he's made deals like this, and some of them have paid off. Sometimes he collects ten for one; sometimes he gets stuck for the amount of his initial investment."

"Well, if he's up on his toes, he isn't going to get stuck for anything on this one," she said. "They should be able to locate the car. The police really should have done so long ago, and once they locate it they can get a big payoff.

"I wasn't born yesterday. This kind of a deal isn't like a deal where somebody runs into you and stops the car and gives you hospital treatment and every aid. This is a case where a person ran into me, knocked me down, then speeded off and left me lying there. That's a crime. The woman who was driving that car could go to prison. Once you find her, she'd pay off . . . and you're representing her. I know that just as well as I'm sitting here. I should make my figure fifty thousand dollars."

I laughed and said, "Go ahead, make it fifty thousand dollars if you want to, and I'll walk right out that door and you'll never see me again—unless you happen to want to subscribe to these magazines, and then the subscription department will take over."

"All right," she said. "I happen to want the money. I'm taking a chance. Ten thousand dollars in cash within twenty-four hours.

"And I'll live up to my bargain. I'll sign any kind of papers you want and I'll be hard to find as far as the police are concerned. I'll let that young woman get off scot free."

I shook my head and said, "We couldn't do that."

"Why not?"

"That would be conspiring to compound a felony," I said.

"Well, suppose I just didn't *say* anything about it?"

"That," I said, "would be perfectly legal, just so we didn't have any understanding along those lines."

She smiled at me, a wise, knowing smile. Then she looked at her watch and said, "Well, young man, if you're going to get action within twenty-four hours, you'd better get started."

"You don't want these magazines?" I asked.

She laughed at me.

I said, "I'll try and get in touch with my party and, in the event he's interested, I'll let you know."

I gently closed the screen door, backed off the porch and walked the two blocks to where I had parked the agency jalopy. I drove another six blocks to a telephone station, rang up Elsie Brand and said, "Send a wire to Clayton Dawson as follows: 'IS IT WORTH TEN GRAND IMMEDIATE CASH? MUST CLOSE DEAL WITHIN TWELVE HOURS.'"

"How do I sign it?" she asked.

"You don't sign it," I said, "and you don't charge it to our account. You go down to the nearest telegraph office, pay for it in cash, and leave a fictitious address."

CHAPTER THREE

I had my answer within two hours, sent from Denver, Colorado, straight wire:

CLOSE DEAL. SEE PHYLLIS ELDON, PARKRIDGE APARTMENTS, NUMBER SIX O NINE. NO PAPERS.

I got to the Parkridge Apartments within thirty minutes after receiving the wire and rang the bell on 609.

Phyllis Eldon was a dish.

If there was any resemblance to her father, I failed to see it. She was a ravishing honey-blond beauty with big, innocent-appearing blue eyes, a peaches-and-cream complexion and apparently all of the standard parts in the deluxe model.

"I'm Donald Lam," I told her.

She said, "I've been expecting you. You want ten grand, don't you?"

"I do."

"She said, "Sit down, please. What do you want—Scotch or bourbon?"

"Neither, at the moment. I'm working."

"My, but you're abstemious. I'm working, myself, but I'm going to have some Scotch and soda."

"Double it," I told her.

She went over to the bar.

It was a nice apartment, all dolled up with fancy gadgets and an air of loud luxury.

She got a couple of crystal glasses, splashed in Scotch, ice, squirted in soda, and brought it over.

"Here's how," she said.

"How," I told her.

"I suppose," she said, "you think I'm a very wicked woman?"

"Are you?" I asked.

"I don't know," she said. "I suppose my father told you a lot of stories about me."

"Trying to pump me?" I asked.

"No," she said, "but I just consider myself a human being, and I'd like to have you look at me the same way."

19

I looked her over and said, "I'm looking at you—and I think you're human."

She laughed at that and said, "I see you can twist words around to suit yourself."

She raised her glass and looked at me over the rim. I bowed to her and we drank.

I could see she was sizing me up.

"My dad says that you're a very high-grade detective."

"That wasn't the way he reacted when he first met me," I said.

"He was disappointed. He thought you'd be a bigger man."

"Sorry, I couldn't accommodate him."

"You look all right to me," she said. "I think you'd be very competent—in a clinch."

Her eyes met mine over the top of the liquor glass and she smiled.

Abruptly her expression changed. "Just what's the pitch, Donald?"

I said, "Mrs. Harvey W. Chester was injured six days ago in a hit-and-run accident. She was struck down in a pedestrian crossing. She has no idea of who hit her except it was a car driven by a girl."

"Go on," she said.

I said, "I asked her about the extent of her injuries and about a settlement."

"Donald, could you settle a case like that without compounding a felony?"

I brushed the question aside and said, "I told her that I knew a person who liked to buy up claims such as hers; that sometimes he bought them up and was able to find the culprit and settle for a very large sum and make a handsome profit; and sometimes he couldn't find the persons responsible and, as a result, had to let the whole thing drop. And, of course, in cases of that sort, he lost out."

She thought that over for a moment, then her eyes looked at me with a new-found respect.

"I'm to buy out the claim?" she asked.

I shrugged my shoulders and said, "If you think it's worth it; it's touch and go. The probabilities are we'll never find the person who drove the car."

"But if we do?"

"Then you'd have an assignment of the claim."

"Wouldn't a document of assignment of that sort be considered . . . well, incriminating?"

"The assignment would be to me," I said. "I'd act as intermediary in case anything came up."

"Wouldn't that be a little risky in case anyone should ask questions?"

"People ask me questions all the time. Sometimes I don't have to give them complete answers."

"You do when the police ask."

"I don't have to tell the names of my clients."

"Donald," she said, "I think you're *wonderfully* competent."

"Thank you."

"Do you want to know what all this means to me?"

"Hell, no!" I told her.

For a moment she flushed, then she laughed and said, "I guess I understand. What you don't know, won't hurt you."

"What I don't know, won't hurt *you*," I said.

"And you don't want to hurt me, do you Donald?"

"You're a client," I said.

She said, "You sit right there."

She walked into the back bedroom. Once I thought I heard hoarse whispering.

She came back carrying one hundred hundred-dollar bills, nice crisp currency.

She counted them out on my lap, her fingers from time to time brushing against my leg as she put the bills down.

"There you are, Donald, one hundred hundred-dollar bills. That's a total of ten thousand dollars. Now, tell me, what'll happen if the police do finally trace the car that hit this woman?"

"They'd ask her to prosecute."

"And if they prosecuted?"

"They might get a conviction, depending on the evidence they had; but if she didn't prosecute, they might have a little trouble."

"And, so far, they have no evidence?"

"They have a dress, from which a piece of cloth was torn; and they probably have glass from the headlight. They usually have something like that."

"One has to take chances these days, doesn't one?" she said, smiling.

"One does," I said.

I put down the empty glass and got up to go.

21

She watched me speculatively. "Donald," she said, "I think you're wonderful—just absolutely *wonderful!*"

I grinned at her and said, "If I started disagreeing with you it would make too long an arguement. Good-bye, Phyllis."

"Goodbye, Donald."

CHAPTER FOUR

I again parked the agency car two blocks from the home of Mrs. Chester, walked back around the big house to the little bungalow in the rear, and knocked on the door.

"Come in," she called, dispiritedly.

I opened the door and went in.

Mrs. Chester was sitting up in bed with big, dark circles under her eyes.

"I've had a terrible night," she said.

"Don't you have anyone staying with you?"

"Can't afford it. I wish I could go to my daughter's place; but she can't come here, and I don't have the money to go there."

"Where does she live?"

"Denver."

"You're feeling pretty bad?"

"I think some of those nerves must have got bruised," she said. "The nerve sheaths, or whatever it is, got injured and they just ache, ache, ache all the time. . . . You ever have a toothache?"

"Yes."

"Well, this is just like a thousand toothaches all up and down your leg; and every time I take a deep breath, I hurt."

"The doctors didn't find any broken bones?"

"No, that's what they said, but I don't know how you're going to depend on a doctor."

"You have to depend on somebody."

"Yes, I suppose you do."

"Don't they give you anything to make you sleep?"

She said, "I've got some sleeping medicine but it doesn't do me much good."

I said, "I've been in touch with the man who sometimes makes settlements in advance. He's willing to take a chance on being able to collect."

She looked at me and her eyes narrowed in speculation. "I've been thinking over the proposition you made," she said. "I'd want twelve thousand five hundred dollars in cold, hard cash."

I shook my head.

23

"Well, that's what I want."

I took out the hundred-dollar bills and spread them on a table. "I'm prepared to give you this much," I said. "Ten thousand dollars. In return for that, you'll guarantee that if at any time we want you to sign papers assigning the claim, you'll sign those papers. If we want you to sign a complaint, you'll sign a complaint; and any money that is recovered as the result of that litigation will go to us. We will, of course, pay all the expenses."

"I can't do it," she said. "It just isn't in the cards. I've been suffering a lot since you left here. I'll tell you what I'll do, I'll make it eleven thousand."

"I'm sorry," I told her, "eleven won't do. I have ten and that's it."

She shook her head obstinately. "Well, you can tell your friend to go jump in the lake. I'm not going to settle for any ten thousand."

"Okay," I said. I gathered up the money.

She sat there watching me.

Her face looked like death.

I put the money in a neat stack, slapped a rubber band around it, put it in my pocket and said, "I'm sorry, Mrs. Chester."

"Who is this man you're working for?" she asked.

"I told you," I said, "he's a sharpshooter. He's a big-shot gambler on cases of this sort. Sometimes he'll make a killing; sometimes he won't."

"The pain is terrible," she said. "I need someone to take care of me."

"I'm sorry."

"How would it be if we made some kind of a time deal? If you gave me a thousand dollars down and then we could go fifty-fifty, or something like that, on what I collected. What I need is money enough to go to my daughter's in Denver."

I shook my head. "I'm only an agent, myself," I said, "and I did this just to accommodate you."

"What do you do for a living?" she asked.

"Suppose we say that I sell magazines?"

"Phooey," she said, and started laughing, a harsh, metallic laugh.

"Well," I told her, "we're not getting anywhere here." And I started for the door.

She waited until I had the door half closed, then she said, "Wait!"

The word was like the crack of a whip.

I kept on closing the door.

I heard her get out of bed.

She came to the door, a pathetic sight, holding herself against the doorknob with one hand and against the jamb with the other.

"Help me!" she said, "I'm going to faint. I got out of bed."

I turned and retraced my steps.

She collapsed as I reached the door.

"Oh, help me!" she said. "Help me! I'm so weak and frail and helpless."

I eased her back toward the bed.

She was moaning and groaning. "Oh, I shouldn't have done it! I shouldn't have done it! The doctor told me not to get up—Oh, my poor nerves."

I eased her down onto the bed.

"That better?" I asked.

She pointed a wan, wobbly finger to a white, round pillbox. "Get me two of those pills with water. Quick!"

I took the cover off the box, got her a glass of water, said, "Take the pills if you want."

She picked out two of the pills, swallowed them with water, lay back, gasping. "Don't go," she said. "Don't leave me."

I drew up a chair and sat down by the head of the bed.

She lay there with her eyes closed for a couple of minutes.

"Are you feeling better now?" I asked.

She gave a wan smile.

"Well," I told her, "I'm going."

"Don't go."

She opened her eyes and spoke with an apparent effort. She said, "You're a good boy. You are only trying to help me, I know that. I need the money—on, *how* I need the money! I need attention. I need to have loving friends around me. I want to get to my daughter in Denver—I'll take it."

"Take what?"

"The ten thousand."

I said, "You'd better wait until you're feeling better."

"No, no, I want to leave. I want to leave right now. I'll get an ambulance to take me to the airplane and they can put me aboard the airplane and I'll be in Denver in the shake of a cat's whisker."

I said, "You'll have to sign a release."

"Of course," she said, "a man isn't going to give a body ten thousand dollars for nothing. Do you have the paper?"

"I have a paper," I said, "showing that for ten thousand dollars you sell, transfer, set over and assign to the Reserve

National Bank, as trustee, all of your claims of any sort, nature and description against any person or persons, known or unknown, who have inflicted any injuries on you during the past year; and, in particular, any persons who may have caused an automobile to collide with you in any way. But generally, and specifically, you include any and all damages you may have for any reason or reasons whatsoever, because of any torts against any person or persons."

"What's a tort?" she asked.

"A civil wrong," I said, "usually accompanied by an act of violence or infringing a person's rights."

"You give me ten thousand dollars and a fountain pen," she said. "I'll sign it. Lift me up in bed a minute, Donald."

I handed her the document and she started to sign it.

"Read it," I said.

"I don't feel quite up to reading just yet."

"All right, then," I said, "I'll come back in the evening when you do feel up to reading."

"No, no, I can read it if I have to. I'm going to be in Denver this evening."

She read through the document laboriously, moving her finger along each line as she read, and moving her lips, formulating each word.

When she had finished, she said, "Hand me the ten thousand."

I handed her the ten thousand dollars and she counted it carefully. Then she signed her name.

"All right," she said, "that does it. . . . Young man, you move that telephone over by my bed. I'm going to get an ambulance and get to the airport. I'm going to make reservations for a ticket."

"Do you think you could sit up on a trip to Denver?"

"I'm certainly going to try it," she said. "They have nice soft, seats and I know the stewardess will let me stretch out on that curved seat at the back, particularly if the plane isn't crowded. I'll take care of myself all right. You'd be surprised how considerate people are of a person who's fragile and has been hurt. . . . You let me have the phone."

"Do you want me to telephone for the ambulance?"

"No, I'll telephone for it when those pills have taken their full effect. After I've taken those pills, I don't feel really bad pain for three or four hours. The doctor told me not to take them any oftener than I had to because they might be habit-forming, but believe you me, young man, I'm going to take them all the way to Denver."

26

I pulled the telephone over to the bed and said, "Is there anything else I can do?"

"Nothing," she said.

I went out to the agency car, got an envelope, put the assignment in it, addressed it to myself at the office, stamped it, dropped it in a mailbox.

Then I sent a wire to our client in Denver: "BELT IS BUCKLED" and signed it *Donald Lam.*

CHAPTER FIVE

When I walked in the office the next morning, there were danger signals flying all over the place. The receptionist held up her hand with the palm out. On the table where incoming mail was placed, there were two baskets—one marked *B. Cool* and one marked *D. Lam.* There were letters in the Lam basket, but on top of the letters was a red paperweight. That was the private danger signal that Elsie Brand had worked out.

Those signals gave me a chance to prepare for trouble. Usually it meant some big husky was threatening to beat me to pulp if I didn't quit the job I was doing.

I braced myself for trouble, opened the door of my private office and walked in.

Sergeant Frank Sellers was sitting there with Elsie Brand, and Sellers was mad.

Sellers was a big, husky, two-fisted dedicated cop, who didn't do very much talking himself and distrusted those who did talk.

Sellers believed in physical action. He wanted to be doing something all the time. He was always in motion. Sometimes he clenched and unclenched his hands. Most of the time he chewed on a soggy, unlit cigar stump.

Now he was both clenching and unclenching his hands and worrying the stump of the cigar.

"Hello, Pint Size," he said, his voice ominous.

"Hello, Sergeant."

"You're in a jam!"

"Me?"

"You."

"How come?"

"Don't play that childlike, cherubic innocence with me. I don't go for it."

"I didn't say I was innocent. I wanted to know what particular charge you are making against me."

"You thought you were pulling a fast one."

I said nothing.

"That hit-and-run business," he said.

I raised my eyebrows.

"A dame by the name of Mrs. Harvey W. Chester who lives in a little old-fashioned bungalow in the rear of 2367 Doorman Avenue."

"What am I supposed to have done with her?"

"That's one of the things you're going to tell me," Sellers said. "This much I know. You knew we were investigating a hit-and-run. You were representing the person who did the hitting and running. You took a nice, fat wad of cold, hard currency out there, squared the deal with her and paid her to disappear.

"Now then, for your information, in case you're too dumb to know it, that's compounding a felony and we don't like to have people compounding felonies."

I sat down beside Elsie's desk. She was looking at me with frightened eyes.

"Got a warrant?" I asked.

"Don't crack smart," he said, "or I'll take you and throw your can in the cooler just to show you what I can do. I've got enough on you to take you in on suspicion right now, but I am giving you a chance to come clean."

"What do you want?"

"I want to know the name of your client."

I shook my head. "That would be violating a professional confidence."

"And if I don't get the name of your client, it'll be violating a state law."

"Who told you all this stuff anyway?" I asked.

"Never mind that," he said, and then added grimly, "*we* don't divulge the sources of *our* information."

"Well, why don't you trace this woman, Mrs. Chester What's-her-name, if you're so smart?"

"Because, by God, you fixed it so we couldn't trace her," Sellers said.

"I did?"

"You know damned well you did! You had an ambulance call at the place, loaded her into that ambulance, had her taken to the airport and put in a wheelchair while she was about half full of dope. You put her on a plane for Denver, and when she got to Denver, she just plain disappeared."

"Oh come, Sergeant," I said, "she had to have a wheelchair meet her when she got off the plane in Denver and—"

"Sure, a wheelchair was there," Sellers said. "She was met by private parties in a private automobile and she vanished into thin air.

"Before she left Los Angeles, she did a little talking, however, and she showed a friend a whole wad of hundred-dollar bills. She paid her rent with a hundred-dollar bill. So help me, she even used a hundred-dollar bill to pay off the ambulance."

"What happened to her baggage?"

"Not a damned piece of baggage, except a little handbag."

"What's left in the house?"

"Nothing, somebody came and cleaned it out. Don't be so damned innocent. I'm just letting you know what we have on you."

"Why does it have to be me?"

"Because you parked your car a couple of blocks away from the house and made a pass of selling magazine subscriptions.

"One woman saw you park your car, get out with the magazines, and then you went to the door and solicited her. She didn't think you looked like a magazine salesman, didn't think your heart was in it, and thought you were casing the joint. So she took the license number of your automobile and phoned it in, asking us to check with the Better Business Bureau.

"Well, those calls are a dime a dozen, but we made the check. Then, when we went out to interview Mrs. Chester and found she'd been masterminded out of existence. I started checking back on things and Communications happened to remember that call.

"I went out and made a door-to-door canvass, personally. I found where you pulled the magazine racket on two other houses and then went to the Chester bungalow in back.

"That was your introduction, all right, the magazine racket. From then on, you played it by ear and you evidently made a pretty damned good job of selling.

"Now then, I'm putting it on the line. I'm not going to penalize Bertha on this thing, because we don't have so much trouble with Bertha. But every damned time you get hold of a case, you start cutting corners, and this time I'm going to have your license."

Sellers lurched to his feet. "Think it over," he said. "Give us the name of your client and let us clean up that hit-and-run case or lose your license."

"And if I give you the name of the client?"

"You've still got a rap for compounding a felony; but, if you'll clip your wings a little bit and not try to fly quite so high, you can probably square that with the D.A."

"Thank you," I said.

"Okay, Pint Size, you're a smart little operator and you're like all these brainy little bastards that get smart. You just get too damned smart.

"We've got a hit-and-run charge and we want to clean it up, and we've got a few clues pointing in the right direction. We may be able to clean it up without any help from you, but that's no skin off your nose. Either you come through with the full story on this, or you lose your license."

"How long have I got?" I asked

"Just long enough to make up your mind," Sellers said. "Not more than twenty-four hours."

Sellers rolled the cigar around from one side of his mouth to the other, glowered at me, said, "You've given me a helping hand once or twice after you've made me walk over hot coals for a mile or two, and you've always been fair about giving me the publicity. That much I appreciate.

"But get this straight." And Sellers reached out and grabbed my necktie and pulled me close to him. "Get this straight, you little bastard, I'm a cop! I'm the law! I'm enforcing the law. I respect the law, and I don't like guys that cut corners with the law! And in case you don't know it, that means Donald Lam!"

Sellers pushed me backward into the chair, let go of my necktie and stomped out.

Elsie Brand looked at me, on the verge of tears. "Did you do it, Donald?"

"Yes."

"Are you going to tell the name of your client?"

"No."

"What are you going to do?"

"I don't know."

"You'll have to tell him, Donald."

"Does Bertha know anything about this?"

"I don't think so. Sellers came stomping right in here."

"Okay," I said, "I'm out for the day, Elsie. If anybody wants me, you don't know where I am and," I told her with a smile, "that's going to be the understatement of the week."

"Donald, will you *please* be careful?"

"It's too late to be careful now," I told her. "Better send to the drugstore, order a package of tranquilizers and deliver them to Bertha."

CHAPTER SIX

I was fortunate in catching a through jet plane to Denver.

The hostess probably thought I was the most surly passenger the line had ever carried. They tried to make things nice for me but I sat there trying to fit pieces of the puzzle together.

We glided over the orange groves of California, gathering altitude; rocketed across the desert; crossed the chain of lakes formed by the Colorado River, and on into the Rocky Mountains.

The scenery was breathtaking, stupendously beautiful, but I sat frowning contemplation and I still couldn't put the puzzle together.

I arrived in Denver, went to a phone booth and looked up the Dawson Re-Debenture Discount Security Company.

There was no listing.

I called Information and asked for a number. There was no number.

I looked at the richly embossed card Clayton Dawson had given me and called the telephone number which was given on the card as the number of the executive offices.

A well-modulated feminine voice answered the telephone simply repeating the number I had called.

I said, "Are these the offices of the Dawson Re-Debenture Discount Security Company?"

"Yes, they are," she said.

"I would like to talk with Clayton Dawson, assistant to the president."

"Just a moment," she said.

There was silence for a moment; then the voice again, crisply efficient, "No, he's not in at the moment. May I take a message, please?"

"When do you expect him in?"

"I'm not able to give out that information. May I ask who's calling?"

"Just an old friend of his," I said. "Purely a social matter. Forget it," and hung up before she could ask more questions.

I called a cab and gave the driver the address on the card.

The office building was there all right; the right floor was there; the room which had been given on the card as presidential head-quarters was there but it said HELEN LOOMIS, *Public Stenographer*; down below appeared, ANSWERING SERVICE, in parentheses; and over on the right was a string of names on the ground glass, mostly mining companies. The name of Dawson Re-Debenture Discount Security Company didn't appear there.

I walked in.

It was a two-room affair, a reception room and an inner office marked *Private*, which could probably be used by any one of the subtenants if he had to have a place for a private conference.

The woman who sat at the reception desk, with an electric typewriter over on the side, was an individual who had pounded out a lot of words in her lifetime. She had washed-out, weary eyes, but she had taken a lot of care of her personal appearance and could have been anywhere from fifty to sixty-five. Her manner was crisply capable.

She was typical of hundreds of thousands of women who had started out as stenographers, became secretaries, married and left the job; then, after a while, these women were widowed and had to go back to work, only to find that the good jobs were no longer available for those who were older and a little "rusty" with their shorthand. But this woman had probably finally secured work by sheer merit and determination, worked herself up, then reached an age where someone decided she was no longer sufficiently decorative and had sent her off to the secretarial junk pile.

The only difference was Helen Loomis hadn't gone to the junk pile. She'd scraped together enough money to get a couple of rooms in an office building; had lined up enough clients to keep her going as a public stenographer; opened a telephone answering service and a mail drop for half a dozen promoters who couldn't afford office space, and probably some fly-by-nights who wanted to do business by mail.

"Miss Loomis?" I asked.

"Yes," she said.

"I understand you have an answering service and furnish office space."

"That's right."

"I'd like to find out a little more about it. I'm thinking of organizing a company here in Denver. What are your rates?"

"That depends entirely upon the type of company, the amount of work, and the number of telephone calls."

I said, "This would probably be limited to not more than one telephone call a day, and not more than thirty letters a month, but I might want to use the private office at times."

She said, "We have this room available for private conferences, and—What was your name?" she asked.

"Lam," I told her. "Donald Lam."

"And what is the nature of your business, Mr. Lam.

"I am an investment counselor," I said. "I would like to begin in a small way."

"Oh, yes, rates would be forty-five dollars a month for putting your name on the door, having an answering service, taking messages and the reasonable use of the private office . . . Of course, you understand I have other clients and, at times, there might be a conflict."

"Thank you," I told her. "I'll think it over and let you know within the next day or two."

"Very well," she said. And then asked, "How did you hear about my service? How did you happen to come to me?"

"One of your clients," I said, "a Clayton Dawson."

Her eyes suddenly hardened. "I thought I recognised your voice. Weren't you the person who called on the telephone and asked for Mr. Dawson?"

"That's right," I said. "I'm an old friend of his and thought I'd let him perform the introductions, if he was in."

"My clients very rarely put in time at the office," she said. "It's used mostly for an answering service."

"You haven't any idea where I could get hold of Clay now?" I asked.

"Clay?" she inquired.

I laughed apologetically. "Clayton Dawson."

"Oh, no, Mr. Dawson was in earlier today, picked up a special delivery letter and went out. I'm sorry, I don't have a home address for him."

"Well," I said, "if he comes in, tell him to be sure to get in touch with his old friend, Donald Lam."

"And where will you be, Mr. Lam?"

I laughed and said, "Clay knows where he can reach me, all right. Clay's the one who is the rolling stone. He's always into something, usually something new. He's the promoter type."

"I see," she said, in a manner which intimated the interview was being terminated.

"I'll get in touch with you if I go ahead with this deal," I said, and walked out.

The Merchants' Credit Association had two Clayton Dawsons, and neither one of them could by any possibility of the imagination be the one I wanted. No one had ever heard of a Dawson Re-Debenture Discount Security Company.

The registrar of voters had several Dawsons but, here again, no one who could be my man, judging from ages.

I went to the car rental agencies and inquired if a Clayton Dawson had rented a car from them within the last two weeks or ten days, and drew blank.

The Clayton Dawson who had called on me was a shadow who had given Denver as a phony background. He had carefully laid his plans so he couldn't be traced.

And Sergeant Frank Sellers was going to take my license unless I came up with the name of my client in forty-eight hours.

If I tried giving Sergeant Sellers the story of what actually happened, he would throw the book at me for being a poor liar and not being able to make up a better story than that.

I took a cab to the airport and found that I had to wait two hours for a plane back to Los Angeles.

CHAPTER SEVEN

I picked an isolated booth at the Denver airport and called Phyllis Eldon in her apartment. Somewhat to my surprise I heard her voice answering the phone.

"This," I said, "is Donald Lam talking."

"Yes, Mr. Lam." Her voice was warm and friendly.

"I'm in a jam."

"I guess everyone gets in a jam sooner or later."

"I'm in a jam on account of you and your father."

"Indeed?"

"I'm in Denver now. I tried to see you father. I can't locate him. I've got to get in touch with him. Do you know where I can find him?"

"No, what's the trouble?"

I said, "I don't want to discuss details over the telephone, but there has been a leak somewhere and certain persons are trying to trace the source of a certain payment. I think if you could meet me at the airport tonight, it might be well for us to have a conference. your father was considerably less than frank with me, and if I'm going to take a rap for you people, I want to have the cards on the table."

"What plane are you coming in on?" she asked.

I gave her the flight number, the airline and the time of arrival.

She said, "I'm not answering for my father, but I'll tell you one thing, I try to be a squareshooter. If a man sticks his neck out for me, I remember it and appreciate it. I'll be there."

"That," I told her, "makes me feel a whole lot better."

"Can you tell me who's causing the trouble?" she asked.

"I'm afraid it's getting to be a *uniform* procedure," I said.

"I don't get you," she said. "A uniform procedure, a—Oh, yes, I get it! All right, Donald, I'll be there. 'Bye now."

Her voice was warm, friendly and seductive.

I killed time until my flight was called, then settled back in cushioned comfort on the plane and relaxed.

What I had found out about Clayton Dawson made me think I had been taken for a ride, but his daughter who was supposed to be wayward, obstinate and independent, impudent, ungrateful, undisciplined and perhaps immoral was turning out to be a regular trouper.

That, I reflected, was the way with the world. Then the stewardess brought me an old-fashioned and ten minutes later I didn't have a care in the world. Everything was going to work out all right.

We arrived in Los Angeles right on schedule and I managed to be in the vanguard of passengers leaving the plane. I was carrying a brief-case and nothing else, travelling light.

I spotted Phyllis standing at the gates. She waved at me with warm spontaneity.

I was just about to wave back when my eyes caught a glimpse of the face of Sergeant Frank Sellers, standing slightly back from the crowd. He was wearing civilian clothes and trying to keep in the background as much as possible.

I gave Phyllis a stony stare, hoping she'd get the idea.

She lowered her arm, her eyes puzzled.

I marched forward, my eyes straight ahead.

Phyllis pushed her way toward me.

I shook my head imperceptibly.

She didn't get it.

"Donald!" she said, grabbing my arm. "Donald, don't you remember me?"

I turned then.

There was no chance as passing it off as a mistake or patching it up in any way. She'd called my name. and the fact that I had quite evidently been trying to avoid her didn't help any. It gave Sellers all the leeway he wanted.

He came swooping down on us like a hawk on a covey of quail.

"Hello, Pint Size!" he said. "Who's your friend?"

Phyllis turned to look at him and said, "Go peddle your papers, big boy, we have a date."

Sellers pulled the leather folder out of his hip pocket, opened it and flashed his star at her.

"You're damned right, we have a date!" he said. "Only it may not be the sort of date you are anticipating with Donald."

"Oh, for God's sake," I said, "are you going to ride herd on my love life, too, Sellers?"

I dropped the brief case, opened my arms and had time to give Phyllis a quick wink.

She melted into my arms and said, "Lover boy!" then raised her lips.

We had a long clinging kiss, and regardless of what her father may have said about her, or thought about her, that girl had a technique that was simply out of this world.

Sellers stood watching us.

I said, "I'll talk with you tomorrow, Frank, but tonight I'm busy. *Very* busy."

Sellers twisted the unlighted cigar in his mouth.

On the outskirts of the crowd, a tall, rather distinguished-looking individual started walking rapidly away.

"Hey, you," Sellers said.

The man kept walking.

"You in the gray suit," Sellers said, "come back here!"

The man paused, looked back over his shoulder, his face showing surprise.

"Come here," Sellers said.

The man came back, his face angry, "What do you mean ordering me around like that?"

Again, Sellers showed him the buzzer. "I wasn't born yesterday;" he said.

"I don't give a damn when you were born," the man said, "don't try to interfere with me. What do you think you're pulling?"

Sellers said, "I think somebody's trying to pull a fast one on me. A red-hot babe like this doesn't go to meet her boy friend at the airport and take a chaperone along. You were with this girl while she was waiting. Now, what's the pitch?"

"Why, we were simply talking. I know Miss Eldon. She's a friend of mine."

"Yeah? And you just met her at the gate here, casually?"

"That's right."

"All right," Sellers said, "what were you doing out here at the gate?"

"I came to meet a friend."

"And what happened to the friend?"

"He didn't come."

Sellers grinned and said, "Don't be silly, they're still getting off the plane. You were trying to make a getaway. Let's take a look • at your driving license. Who are you, anyway?"

The man said, "My name is Colton C. Essex, and for your information, I'm an attorney at law."

"Well, well, well," Sellers said, "I guess maybe we're beginning to hit pay dirt. And how did you come out to the airport, Mr. Essex?"

"I don't know as that's any of your business."

"I'm making it my business," Sellers said.

He turned to Phyllis. "And how did *you* come out to the airport?"

"I drove out in my car."

"That's fine," Sellers said, "we'll go take a look at your car."

"A look at my car!" she said. "What do you mean? It's *my* car. Are you by any chance, intimating that I've stolen a car?"

People were beginning to form a ring around us now, and I knew there was no use trying to carry it any farther.

"Okay, Sergeant," I said, "if that's the way you feel about it, we'll go take a look at her car."

"And we'll be damned sure it's *her* car," Sellers said.

"You want my claim check?" she asked, handing it to him.

"You're damned right, I want it," Sellers said. "Come on, let's go! . . . You, too, Essex. Come along!"

We walked out to the airport to the parking lot, and a crowd of curiosity seekers followed us part way; then began to melt away as we left the building and walked across to the parking lot. A couple of them, however who were more persistent, tagged along behind, talking in low voices and looking—doubtless wondering what super criminals had been flushed by the police.

Sellers was feeling very, very well pleased with himself.

"The next time you start out on a secret mission, Pint Size," he said, "don't use the air travel card of Cool and Lam to buy your ticket."

Phyllis said, "I wish you'd either light that cigar or throw it away."

"If he lights it," I told her, "it stinks."

"Then throw it away," she said.

Sellers was feeling so good he took the soggy cigar stump out of his mouth and tossed it away. "Anything to oblige a lady," he smirked.

It didn't take Sellers long to locate Phyllis' car, nor to check the registration and look at the dent on the right front fender.

"How d'you do this?" he asked.

"Heavens, I don't know," she said. "It was done somewhere in a parking lot."

Sellers took a magnifying glass from his pocket and looked the fender over.

"What in the world are you trying to do?" she said.

Sellers said, "Where were you two headed for your smooching?"

"Does it make any difference?"

"It may make quite a bit of difference," Sellers said. "So far,

I'm giving you a break. If you were going to your apartment, I'll go there with you and we'll do the questioning there. But if you want to get technical about it, we can do the questioning someplace else."

"We'll go to my apartment," she said.

"All right, Essex," Sellers said with a grin, "you wanted to meet a friend and we don't need to detain *you* any longer."

"It's too late now," Essex said, "my friend has left. I'll ride along uptown with you."

"I didn't invite you," Sellers said.

"Well, I did," Phyllis said, "and if you're going to question me in any way, I'm going to have my attorney along."

"This your attorney?" Sellers asked.

"He is now," she said.

Seller grinned. "All right," he said, "let's go."

The ride up to the Parkridge Apartments was made in silence. Phyllis drove the car competently and was very, very careful to keep within all the speed limits and traffic regulations.

Frank Sellers was doing a lot of thinking.

Phyllis parked the car and we took the elevator up to her apartment.

Sellers said, "You have a driving license as Phyllis Dawson. Your name here is Phyllis Eldon. What's the idea?"

"Dawson," she said, "is my official name, but Eldon is my professional name."

"What profession?"

"I'm studying art."

"Any pictures around?"

She opened the closet door and took out a couple of canvases that looked very much as though she had painted them at random with a squirt gun.

"What are those supposed to represent?" Sellers asked.

"Interpretive paintings," she said. "I paint the emotions."

"What emotion does this one portray?"

"Frustration."

"By God, you said it," Sellers said. "That's the only one of those smears I've ever seen that had an appropriate title."

"Don't you call my painting a smear!" she blazed at him. "In fact, I'm taking altogether too much from you as it is.

"Tell me, Colton, do I have to put up with this?"

"You certainly do not," the attorney said. "An officer is supposed to be a gentleman. He's supposed to investigate cases in his official capacity with some due regard to the rights of the witnesses with whom he is talking."

"All right, all right," Sellers said, "my mistake. I let my tongue slip a little bit. It's a very nice painting, Miss Eldon. Now, if everybody will sit down and be comfortable, I'm going to tell you a few things about my own particular brand of frustration."

"That's all right," Phyllis said, "make yourself right at home, Sergeant."

We sat down.

Sellers said, "Up in the northern part of the city, about a week ago, a Mrs. Harvey W. Chester, a middle-aged woman, was knocked down by a car that sped away and left her lying in the crosswalk.

"She was pretty badly bruised and battered but apparently no bones were broken. A report was made to the traffic department and there was more or less of a routine investigation.

"We went to the scene of the accident. Some cloth had been torn from her dress.

"We felt bad about it, because we don't like to have hit-and-run drivers get away. It isn't the most serious hit-and-run case we've ever had, by a long ways, but it's the principle of the thing."

Sellers stopped, looked around, fished a cigar from his pocket, put it to his mouth, and Phyllis Dawson said sharply, "Not in here!"

"What do you mean, not in here?"

"No cigar smoking in this apartment," she said.

Sellers hesitated awhile, took a deep breath, removed the cigar from his mouth, put it back in his pocket.

"Sometimes on these hit-and-run things," he went on, "the party responsible tries to square things behind the back of the police and then if we find out who's responsible we don't have a complaining witness.

"We don't like to have that happen.

"Donald Lam here is a private detective, and he's a smart operator, I'll say that for him.

"We just happened to find by accident that Donald appeared on the scene, and about the time he appeared on the scene, Mrs. Harvey W. Chester disappeared from the scene and she disappeared with a whole sheaf of hundred-dollar bills. She was happy as a lark.

"The evidence certainly indicates that she not only got a settlement for any physical damages she might have received, and a settlement of her lawsuit, which would have been a civil matter;

but that there was also an attempt made to square any criminal charge which might have been found—and that's compounding a felony.

"I have pretty good evidence that Donald Lam paid over the money. I think he has a receipt somewhere. I've given him a deadline within which to tell the name of his client or have charges made against him which will result in a revocation of his license.

"Now then, what have *you* folks got to say?"

Phyllis started to say something, but Colton Essex beat her to it.

"Nothing," he snapped.

"What do you mean?" Sellers said.

"I mean nothing," Essex said.

"All right, then I'll go at it the hard way," Sellers said.

He walked over to the telephone, picked up the instrument, dialed headquarters, said, "I'm at the Parkridge Apartments, in six o nine. There's a car down here, a this year's model Cadillac with a dent in the fender. It's in the building parking lot. The license number is ODT 067. I think it's the car that was involved in that hit-and-run case with Mrs. Harvey W. Chester a while ago.

"Get a tow car out here; pick up that car; take it down to the police laboratory, go over it with a magnifying glass, and in particular see if you can't find some threads which match the dress the Chester woman was wearing at the time she was hit.

"I want that done right away."

Sellers listened for a moment, said, "That's right."

He hung up the telephone, turned to Phyllis and said, "We're impounding your car as evidence. You may have it back when we've had an opportunity to examine it thoroughly. Right now, there are suspicious circumstances and we're holding it."

"Can he do that?" Phyllis asked Colton Essex.

"He's done it," the lawyer said.

"Now then," Sellers went on, "since the party is evidently going to get rough, I'm going to tell all of you a few things. There are several crimes involved here. One is a hit-and-run, in addition to reckless driving and perhaps driving while intoxicated. Another one is compounding a felony, and that's a serious crime in itself."

Seller turned to me. "And in your case," he said, "there's a refusal to co-operate with the police by withholding evidence in a criminal matter."

"What do you mean, withholding evidence?" Colton Essex asked.

"You heard me," Sellers said.

"I heard you state that you had given Donald Lam a time limit within which to divulge the name of his client."

Sellers looked at him, "You heard right," he said.

"Has the time limit expired?" Essex asked.

"Not yet," Sellers admitted, after a moment of awkward silence. "However, when it runs out, I'm going to throw the book at this pint-sized smart aleck."

"But if he tells you within the time limit you're going to let him off the hook?"

Sellers debated with himself. "Well, I guess that's implied.."

Essex looked at me. "Self preservation is the first law of nature," he said. "Go ahead and tell him, Lam."

I glanced at Phyllis.

She nodded.

"My client," I said, "was a man who told me his name was Clayton Dawson and he gave me an address in Denver. It turns out that the address in Denver was just a mail drop and apparently a blind. I've been unable to find Clayton Dawson. All I know about him is that he told me he was assistant to the president of the Dawson Re-Debenture Discount Security Company of Denver, Colorado. There is no such company.

"He told me that his daughter was Phyllis Dawson; that she was going under the name of Phyllis Eldon.

"Now then, you know as much as I do."

"What did you do with Mrs. Chester?" Sellers asked.

"That," I said, "is an entirely different matter. I kept my nose clean on that."

"Did you pay her any money?"

"Yes."

"With the understanding that she wouldn't press any charges?"

"Good heavens, no," I said. "I paid her money because my client wanted to buy up her claim for damages so that he could underwrite any recovery she might make."

"And your client was Phyllis Dawson here?"

"My client," I said, "was Clayton Dawson."

Sellers creased his forehead in a frown.

Essex said. "Now, Lam has told you the name of his client. That is with the consent of Phyllis Dawson, the client's daughter. That purges Lam of any wrongdoing. You haven't a thing in the world against him."

"The hell I haven't," Sellers said. "Don't think that this pint-sized little bastard—"

"Watch your language," Essex snapped.

43

Sellers glowered at him, said, after a moment, "I'm also putting you on my list."

"You be mighty careful I don't put *you* on mine," Essex said.

Sellers took a deep breath, fished a cigar from his pocket.

"Uh, uh," Phyllis said.

Sellers put the cigar back, said, "I could question you folks at headquarters in a more friendly atmosphere. That is, friendly to me."

"It would be a mistake," Essex told him.

"Don't kid yourself. I can still prove that somebody pulled a big hush-hush on a hit-and-run charge and got the victim out of the state."

"What hit-and-run charge?" Essex asked.

"What hit-and-run charge, why, uh, Mrs. Chester, of course."

"Now, there again," Essex said, "you interest me. As an officer you know that hearsay evidence isn't admissible. You have witnesses who saw her being struck and can identify the car?"

"We can't identify the car," Sellers slowly said, "but we think we're going to be able to make identification after the lab gets done with Phyllis Dawson's car."

"Witnesses who saw her being struck down by the car?" Essex asked.

"Witnesses who saw the poor woman lying there moaning in the middle of the crosswalk, trying to get up just after the car had passed."

"And how did they know she was the victim of a hit-and-run driver?"

"Mrs. Chester told them what had happened."

Essex grinned.

"All right, all right," Sellers said, "so it's hearsay, but it isn't going to be hearsay when we get hold of Mrs. Chester.

"Now then, I'm going to tell you smart alecks something, all of you! The department likes to get hold of these hit-and-run drivers and button the case up. That's a matter of policy.

"This case is going to be a lot more than a matter of policy. I'm going to turn this city upside down. I'm going to find Mrs. Chester *if* I find any evidence on that car we've impounded."

"When does my client get her car back?" Essex asked.

"There are two ways of getting it back," Sellers said. "The first one is that you can get a court order; the second one is that you can wait until we get done with it."

Sellers lurched to his feet, turned to me and said, "And as far as you're concerned, Lam, when I get this case solved, if you've cut one single corner, you're going to be selling insurance or engaging in some other activity that will keep you out of *my* hair."

"Perhaps you'd buy a policy from me?" I suggested.

Sellers jerked a cigar from his pocket, shoved it in his mouth defiantly, strode to the door and walked out.

It was several seconds after the door slammed before anybody said anything. Then I said to Phyllis, "Just where is your father?"

She shook her head. "I couldn't tell you."

"Because you don't know?"

"Because I couldn't tell you."

"Couldn't or wouldn't?"

"Couldn't."

Essex said, "You're in the clear, Lam. That was a clever stunt, getting an assignment— Of course, as a lawyer, I can tell you there's some question about the validity of the assignment under the circumstances."

"I was carrying out orders," I said, "I'm not a lawyer."

Essex grinned. "Dawson wanted a *really* good detective. He was a little disappointed in you when he first saw you, but I think you're filling the bill admirably. I'm glad it's happened that way. I feel completely justified."

"Wait a minute!" I said. "*You* feel completely justified! Are you the one who recommended our firm to Dawson?"

He smiled knowingly. "A lawyer can't tell anything about his conversations with his clients without being guilty of unethical conduct. If you have any more trouble, let me know, Lam."

I took it that was a dismissal and said, "Okay, thanks.... I still think there's something in the background in this case."

Essex said unctuously, "Virtually all cases have backgrounds. Human emotions, you know. The interplay of character, conflicting interests and sometimes complex motivations."

"Yes," I said, "complex motivations. . . . And a good night to both of you."

No one saw me to the door.

CHAPTER EIGHT

The next morning when I entered the office Bertha Cool was on the warpath.

"What in blue hell have you been getting into?" she asked.

"Me?"

"You!"

"Nothing, why?"

"Don't hand me that line! Frank Sellers is really gunning for you this time. You're losing your license."

"Who says I'm losing my license?"

"Frank Sellers, for one."

"Phooey!" I said. "He's got nothing on me. He took two and two and added them together and made sixteen. He thinks I covered up a hit-and-run case, compounded a felony and a few other things. But it's all surmise on his part, and—"

"Surmise on his part, my eye!" Bertha interrupted, her little pig eyes glittering like diamonds. "You got suckered into a deal, got your neck stuck way out and Sellers might have protected us if you'd gone to him and put the cards on the table.

"Sellers tells me he gave you a chance.

"But did you take it? Not you! You were smart. You went traipsing off to Denver, to tell our client to get under cover and stay under cover. You made a pay-off in a hit-and-run case with the understanding that there wouldn't be any prosecution.

"And don't tell me that's all a figment of Seller's imagination. You know something?"

"What?" I asked.

"When they took that car of Phyllis Dawson's down to the police lab and checked it over, they found three distinctive threads caught in the spring shackle. When they compared those threads with the torn dress Mrs. Chester had been wearing at the time she was struck down in the intersection, they found they had a perfect match on fibers.

"Let that glib lawyer the Dawsons have retained try to explain that away in front of a jury."

"They impounded the dress that Mrs. Chester was wearing at the time?" I asked.

"No, they didn't," she said, "but they took a sample from the hem."

"How come?" I asked.

"Mrs. Chester was picked up there in the intersection; she was loaded into an ambulance and taken to the hospital. She was suffering from shock, and the doctors warned her she was going to be mighty sore for a few days and would have to stay in bed. Fortunately, she had no bones broken.

"Since it was a hit-and-run case and they saw a tear in her dress, and, apparently, a little strip of cloth that had been gouged out of it by the automobile, the police took a small piece of the material from the inside of the hem."

"Did they get her permission?"

"How the hell do I know?" Bertha blazed. "The police aren't on trial here; *you* are! It's routine in hit-and-run cases to pick up all the physical evidence they can get and salt it away.

"Having got rid of Mrs. Chester, the authorities might have had some trouble if it wasn't for this circumstantial evidence, the dent on the fender, the fibers adhering to the shackle bolt, or whatever it is they call that part of the car. I think Frank Sellers said it was a shackle bolt."

"So Sellers told you all about it?"

"He told me enough about it," she said, "so that I wouldn't need to get mixed up in it and have *my* license revoked along with *yours*. Sellers has been a damned good friend of mine."

"I've been a good friend of his," I said. "I've done a lot for him."

"You've done it in such a manner that it irritates the hell out of him."

"I can't help how he feels. I've done it, haven't I?"

"You've done it. Now you're in a jam. There's only one thing you can do."

"What?"

"Beat Sellers to the punch and don't say that I told you so!"

"You mean with Mrs. Chester?"

"I mean with Mrs. Chester. You gave her money. She took an ambulance to the airport. Apparently, she got aboard a plane for Denver. Something happened to her when she got to Denver. They had a wheelchair ordered for her, but someone must have spirited her out of the terminal. You have two guesses as to who that someone was."

"Meaning our client?"

47

"Meaning *your* client," Bertha said. "Fry me for an oyster, but I'd love to get my claws into him again!"

I said nothing.

"That goddam client," Bertha went on, "just framed you in a picture. He laid a trap and baited it with a little money. Then he made damned certain he couldn't be traced.

"You know something?"

"What?"

"Sellers thinks that this Phyllis Dawson is a complete phoney; that she's not the guy's daughter at all; that she's the guy's mistress; and he's a rich guy, standing between her and ever being brought to account on this hit-and-run charge."

I shoved my hands down deep in my pocket and slumped down in the chair.

"All right," Bertha said after a while, "say something!"

"I'm thinking."

"You're thinking too damned late. You should have done your thinking before you stuck your neck in a noose. I'm going to miss you as a partner, but you sure as hell are going to lose your license over this one, and Sellers is mad. I've never seen him so mad.

"He's told me that they've put thirty detectives on the trail of Mrs. Chester. They're going to find her."

"Perhaps," I said. "But he can't go after me."

"What do you mean he can't go after you?"

"He gave me a deadline to tell him the name of my client. He said in the presence of witnesses that if I told him the name of the client he'd turn off the heat."

"No, he didn't," Bertha said. "He told me you tried to trip him into doing that, but he told you that if you'd cut one little corner he'd throw the book at you. He says you cut a corner. You told him the name of the client but you still compounded a felony.

"He says if you produce Mrs. Chester before noon today, he'll be a lot more lenient with you, but he isn't going to stand for any detective agency going around compounding felonies."

I said, "I can't produce her. I don't know where she is."

"Sellers will find her," Bertha said.

After a while I said, "The case doesn't add up. It doesn't make sense."

"What do you mean?"

I said, "Let's begin at the beginning. This wasn't too serious a hit-and-run case. The woman was struck in a pedestrian crossing, but there were no bones broken. That isn't as though we were dealing with a corpse.

"Now then, mysterious people rush into the act with a lot of money, more money perhaps than Mrs. Chester could ever have recovered. We got money to go and call on the victim. It has to be hushed up right away and fast. I get an opportunity to settle for ten grand and wire our client.

"There isn't even so much as a quibble. My judgment isn't questioned. No one suggests that I try to get the amount whittled down. Whoever is back of this tossed the ten grand in my lap, fast."

"I know what you're getting at," Bertha said. "That means someone who was important was driving the car."

"Provided there was a car," I told her.

"What?" Bertha asked.

I said, "How do we know there was a car?"

"What are you talking about?"

I said, "The whole damned thing is too pat.

"How did Frank Sellers get on my trail so fast? How did he know that Mrs. Chester had been paid money to forget the whole thing?"

"Because Mrs. Chester blabbed. She showed money to her neighbor."

"And how did it happen that Sellers called on the neighbor?"

"He was investigating the case."

"And how did it happen that a man of Seller's stature in the police department started investigating the case?"

"Because it was . . . important."

"It wasn't important at that time," I said. "It wasn't important until he got the lead on a cover-up of compounding a felony—provided there ever was any felony."

"It was a hit-and-run," Bertha said.

"All right," I said, "let's concede for the sake of the argument that it was a hit-and-run. How did Sellers get on the job, personally and get there so fast?"

"I don't know," Bertha said. "Frank Sellers doesn't confide in me."

"There's only one way he got on the job that fast," I said. "He got a tip from someone."

"And who is the someone?" Bertha Cool asked.

I sat there in the chair, thoughtfully silent.

"Well?" Bertha Cool asked, "who was it?"

"Under the circumstances," I said, "it had to be one of three people—No, one of four people."

49

"Who?"

"Either our client, Clayton Dawson, or his so-called daughter, Phyllis, or Sidney Eldon, the boy friend of Phyllis, or Colton Essex, the attorney. . . . And we don't know there really is a Sidney Eldon."

"Are you completely crazy?" Bertha asked. "None of those people would have done it. They were the ones who stood to lose everything."

I got to my feet and said, "I'm going to be out all day, and I may be out for several days."

"You can say that again," Bertha said. "You're out, period. I'm not going to monkey with anyone who is losing his license. Sellers told me to get out from under. I'm getting out."

"Okay," I told her, as I walked out, "the partnership is dissolved."

I went down to my private office.

Elsie Brand had been crying.

"What's the trouble, Elsie?" I asked.

"Bertha told me."

"About the license?"

"Yes."

"Forget it," I told her.

"It means the end of the partnership; it means the end of your career."

"They haven't got my license yet," I said.

"Donald, I couldn't stay on here for a minute without you—you know that."

"Don't sell me short," I said.

She looked at me with warm eyes. "I've *never* sold you short, Donald," she said, "but this time the cards are stacked against you and Bertha is on the warpath. She should have more loyalty as a partner," Elsie blazed. "I could *never* work under her!"

"You're not going to have to," I said. "Stick around and be where I can reach you on the phone. I'm going to be out for a while."

"Where can I reach you in case—in case any real emergency should turn up?" she asked.

"You can't," I told her. "I'll call in from time to time."

"Donald, please—*please* be careful."

"It's too late to be careful now," I told her. "I'm dealing either with a crooked lawyer, a jealous boy friend, a scheming daughter, one hell of a wealthy father, or a combination of any number of them.

"You can't be careful when you go up against a combination of that sort."

"You could at least try," she said, and watched me with anxious eyes as I walked out of the office.

51

CHAPTER NINE

Frank Sellers was a square cop. He was also opinionated, bigoted, not too quick on the uptake, suspicious of any glib talker, and possessed of a bulldog tenacity.

Sellers had the jump on me when it came to finding Mrs. Harvey W. Chester.

I knew that by this time every directory in the city had been searched; every Chester had been contacted, questions had been asked about whether they had a relative named Harvey Chester or knew of a widow, a Mrs. Harvey Chester.

In short, all the ordinary avenues had been plugged.

If I tried to follow the ordinary trails, I'd be trailing along behind, following a beaten path that had been flattened by the feet of a whole bunch of cops.

I had to find some angle of approach which the police officers hadn't thought of as yet.

Mrs. Chester had received ten thousand bucks. She had had an ambulance call and pick her up. She had gone to the airport. She had been placed aboard a plane for Denver.

When she arrived in Denver, a wheelchair was waiting for her. A solicitous gentleman had taken over and wheeled her to a car. She had vanished completely from that instant. The stewardess who had helped her said she was full of dope.

It was a cinch Sellers had been in touch with the Denver police and every attempt was being made to locate Mrs. Chester at that end.

The plane had made one intermediate stop at Las Vegas.

There was no possibility a wheelchair case could have disembarked at Las Vegas without the stewardess knowing it.

There was one other possibility.

The woman who arrived at the Los Angeles airport by ambulance didn't necessarily *have* to be the same one who had got off the plane at Denver. A wheelchair could have been ordered for a Mrs. Harvey W. Chester; and an entirely different Mrs. Harvey W. Chester could have purchased a ticket, switched places on the plane before it took off and while the stewardesses were busy checking incoming passengers.

The woman who boarded the plane could have got off at Las Vegas, having switched her through ticket to a woman who had boarded the plane at the same time that she did.

This would, of course, mean there had been a complete flimflam, but those things have been encountered, particularly in automobile accident cases.

The thing that bothered me was how Frank Sellers could have been so hot on the trail as soon as the money had been paid. It meant there had been a tip-off, probably by an anonymous telephone call, and the way I sized the situation up that telephone call must have been made by Mrs. Harvey W. Chester, by Phyllis, Phyllis' father, a jealous boy friend, or an attorney who was playing a pretty smart game.

This time when I flew to Las Vegas I didn't make the mistake of using the agency air travel card. I dug down in my pocket and paid the fare in cash.

Once on the ground I relied on taxicabs, but I was careful to register at a hotel under my own name.

I started covering the gambling joints.

Las Vegas, Nevada, is a twenty-four-hour-a-day proposition. Night and day the air-conditioned casinos are busy with the rattle of chips, the whir of the slot machines, the voice of the barker announcing that such-and-such a machine has just hit a jackpot, the sound of the ivory ball on the roulette wheel.

Hundreds, thousands of people were going about the business of winning or losing money with grim-faced intensity. I looked the places over. I seldom saw a smile or heard laughter. Persons stood shoulder to shoulder, grim, tense, unsmiling.

Looking for a single face in this aggregation of tourist gambling devotees and curiosity seekers was almost like searching for the proverbial needle in a haystack.

However, someone has said that good police work is ninety per cent legwork and ten per cent head work. That may or may not be true, but I didn't have any alternative. I had to start sifting through Las Vegas.

At that, luck was with me. I went into the Blue Dome Casino, after having spent two hours going from place to place scanning the tense faces of the so-called pleasure seekers, and there she was, big as life, standing in front of a twenty-five-cent slot machine and working the handle like mad.

I moved up behind her.

The man who was playing the machine on her right finally gave up, and Mrs. Chester took over both machines, putting in quarters and jerking down the handles just as fast as she could feed coins into the machine.

I said, "I'm glad to see that you've made such a complete recovery, Mrs. Chester."

She whirled around to face me, her eyes got big, her jaw dropped.

"For God's sake," she said.

"Having any luck?" I asked.

She showed me a bag full of quarters. "Winnings," she said.

"Why did you blow the whistle?" I asked.

"*Me* blow the whistle! Are you nuts?"

I said, "Somebody did. Right at the moment, you're badly wanted. The cops in Los Angeles and Denver are looking for you. They haven't tried Las Vegas yet, but they will."

"Oh, my God," she said.

I just stood there.

"Let's get the hell out of here," she said, "before somebody spots me."

We walked out.

"Got a car?" I asked.

"No," she said.

"Where are you staying?"

"I'm holed up in a little cottage up here, a string of cottages that they rent to people who are here for the six-weeks' residence necessary to get a divorce. The rents are higher than a frightened cat's back, but one has complete privacy."

"Let's take a look," I said.

We went to the motel-type bungalow in a taxicab. Neither of us said anything in front of the driver, but I could see she was sizing me up. She was cautious and she was scared stiff.

The little bungalow was a regular heartbreak house, drab on the outside, furnished with the bare necessities on the inside, a threadbare carpet, overstuffed chairs that looked fairly inviting but were uncomfortable once you sat down.

Six weeks of living in a place of that sort would drive a woman nuts.

Of course, the women who lived there weren't supposed to stay in the house. They would unpack their suitcases, hang their clothes in the closets which were just beginning to get a slight smell of mildew, and then go out into the casinos and on long weekend parties.

Usually the women had boy friends who had more or less actively participated in the bust-up of the marriage. Sometime during the six-week period, these boy friends would get lonely and come flying in to Las Vegas.

If they didn't have boy friends, it was very easy to acquire some. Usually it was the wife who had to qualify for the six-weeks' residence and get the divorce. The husband was too busy making a living for the "family".

We settled down in the living room, so-called, and Mrs. Chester gave me a rather vague smile. "Well," she said, "what do you want?"

I said, "You knew I was coming to call on you before I arrived, didn't you?"

She thought that over for several seconds, then nodded.

"You knew my name?"

"You had been described to me."

"By whom?"

"Do you have to know that?"

"Yes."

"I don't think I can tell you that."

"That," I said, "might be just too bad," and then added after a moment, "for you."

"I had no business getting mixed into this," she said. "I had retired."

"It's a little late to think of that now, isn't it?" I asked.

"I suppose so," she said.

I remained silent.

After a while, she said, "What do you want to know?"

"Who engineered the deal?"

"The attorney."

"Colton Essex?"

"Yes."

"What's your connection with him?"

"I hadn't had any until this came up."

"But you'd known him before?"

"Yes."

"How?"

"He'd been on the other side of one of my cases."

"What do you mean, the other side?"

"He represented the defendant."

"An insurance company?"

"An insurance company and an owner together, yes."

"And what happened?"

"The case was settled for a very small amount."

"What kind of a case was it?"

"One of my usual cases," she said. And then added after a moment, "I'm a professional tumbler. That is, I used to be before I got a little old and a little heavy, but I'm still good.

"I could smack the bumper of an automobile with my handbag, spin away from the car, fall to the ground, roll over and just about any spectator would swear the automobile had crashed into me."

"Even if the automobile wasn't moving?"

"I specialized in moving automobiles," she said. "I'd get in a crosswalk. I'd park my car so that it was a little difficult to see around it and about one car out of ten would cut around my car and go through the crosswalk. I'd size up the car, and naturally I only picked the more expensive makes."

"And then?"

"Then," she said, "I'd have a friend standing by who'd phone for an ambulance before anyone thought to telephone for the police. The ambulance service gets there, picks me up and whisks me away. My friend sees to it that the accident is reported. My address is given. An officer usually comes to check my statement.

"If the party who hits me stops, and there's a report of the accident, I can usually make a deal with an insurance company. If the party who hits me drives away and makes a hit-and-run out of it, we trace the party and get a whale of a settlement because he's so vulnerable. He's mixed up in a hit-and-run and he has to pay through the nose. I use different names each time."

"And Colton Essex knew all about this?"

"I told you he was on the other side of one of my cases. He smelled a pretty big rat, and by the time we got done I had to take a much smaller settlement than is usually the case. He's a good lawyer."

"So then, what happened this time?"

"On this particular night," she said, "my telephone rang. It was Essex. He told me to be at a certain intersection within ten minutes and to put on my act. He said there'd be a settlement of ten grand and I could keep half of it. You couldn't ask for anything better than that."

"Did he tell you what car to pick?"

"Bless you, yes. He told me to pick his car."

"*His* car?" I exclaimed.

"That's right. He said he'd blink the headlights just before he came to the intersection. I was to put on a good act for the benefit of any bystanders, and he would make a clean getaway, but he warned me not to stage the accident until he blinked his head-lights. He wanted a clear field for a getaway."

"Well, I'll be damned," I said.

She said, "It *was* funny, wasn't it?"

"And you were there, and he blinked his headlights?" I asked.

"Bless you," she said, "he went through that intersection ten times before the coast was clear and he blinked his headlights and I strutted my stuff and he speeded up to get away from there; went screaming around the corner, and that was it."

"What about the dress you were wearing?"

"He came to the house afterwards, took some pliers and tore a little piece out of the dress."

"And then?" I asked.

"Then he told me to wait and that, in the course of time, a man would call on me to make a settlement.

"About forty-eight hours later, he called me and said that the man who was coming to call on me would be pretty clever; that he was rather young, slight in build, but quick-thinking and brainy and I wasn't to try and embellish anything, just act dumb. He said you'd put on some sort of an act, but there'd be ten grand in it and I could keep half of it."

"And the other half?"

"I turned it over to the attorney."

I sat there thinking that over.

"Now then," she said, "what are you going to do? Are you going to get rough with me about that five grand? I'm telling you, it's the first decent job I've had for six months. These damned insurance companies have *modus operandi* files on people who fake injuries and you have to keep thinking up something new all the time. In fact, it's getting so that I very seldom press charges any more against people who stop."

"What happens when that occurs?" I asked.

"Oh," she said, "they stop and ask me how badly I'm hurt, and my friend says he's called an ambulance and they give me a card and tell me they're insured and to get in touch with them; that they're reporting the accident to their insurance company, and ask me for my name. Under those circumstances, I usually give them a phony name and address, and they never hear any more about it.

"The people who try to get away, the hit-and-run people—and I'm pretty damned good at sizing up the people who have been drinking—in fact, sometimes my friends help me pick the sucker."

"How?"

"Oh, he goes into a club or saloon, finds the people who are drinking pretty heavy; goes out to the parking station, gets the license number of their automobile and the address from the registration slip so that he knows which direction the guy will be heading when he leaves the bar, and I plant myself at a nearby intersection.

"Of course, that way we miss lots of them, but when we get them, we get them good. You know how it is, a man has been in a bar drinking for an hour and a half, comes out, gets in his car and hits a pedestrian at a cross-walk. He stops if he has to, but if there's any chance for a getaway he steps on it and is long gone.

"Of course, we pick the right times when there isn't much traffic and it's a virtual invitation to an alcoholic driver to step on it and get out of the way."

"How many jobs have you done for Essex?" I asked.

"Bless your soul, this is the only one, and it was a nice clean job."

"Who's the girl who was supposed to have been driving the car, Phyllis Dawson or Eldon? Do you know anything about her?"

"Not a thing. Of course, she wasn't driving any car that I had anything to do with. Colton Essex was driving that car. It was his own car."

"Did you dent it up any?"

"No, I just put my hand on the fender, did a double spin, a flip and a roll."

"Your friend was in on this?"

"No, Essex specifically told me to handle it alone. He said to let the bystanders call the ambulance and if I reported it to the police, I was to report that I was badly shaken up.

"Of course," she went on, "I've got all the symptoms down pat. The symptons of concussion, spinal injury, nerve damage, lack of co-ordination, terrific headaches, backaches, double vision; all that sort of thing."

"You've been coached on the proper symptoms?" I asked.

"And how," she said.

I got up and started pacing the floor. "This is the damnedest thing," I told her.

"Isn't it?" she said. "Now, you look like a nice boy, Donald, and you were awfully nice to me—what are you going to do about all this?"

"I don't know," I told her.

"Going to turn me in?"

"No," I told her, "not now, anyway. I want to find out what's back of it."

Her eyes glittered. "I'll bet you're thinking what I am."

"What?"

"There's money back of it. You take a big-time lawyer like Colton Essex, and he isn't going to get mixed up in monkey business for peanuts. You take a man who's willing to face a hit-and-run rap, pay ten grand, and I only have to kick back half of it, and he's heeled.

"Of course, where I fell down was in letting myself get found. The stipulation was that I was to be hard to find and if anybody located me, I was on my own. Nobody would admit anything, and of course, with my record, I'd wind up behind bars. Nobody would take my word on a stack of Bibles. I guess Essex figured that but, even so, there's money involved here. I can smell it.

"When you've been in the racket the way I have, Donald, you get so you can just smell money, and I'd like to make a deal with you."

I shook my head. "No deal."

Her face showed disappointment. "After the way I've put the cards on the table with you, that's not very fair."

"You put the cards on the table with me because you had to," I told her. "I've found you. All I have to do is report where you are to the police and your happy days are over."

She sighed. "I guess you've got the whip hand," she said, "and I know what that means."

"What?"

"You're going after all that money alone—and damn me, I think you're smart enough to get it."

"How are you doing over here?" I asked.

"Not too bad," she said. "Of course, you can't hit this thing steady and come out ahead. You're fighting a mathematical percentage.

"Whenever I've made a killing I set aside ten per cent of the take, and I come over here and play with it. If I win, I take my winnings and get out. If I lose, when I come to the end of the ten per cent, I'm long gone—that's the only way to beat the game. I can win everything that's on the table if I get lucky, but they can't win over ten per cent of my take from me no matter how lucky they get."

"That's smart," I told her.

"When your dealing with a mathematical percentage, you have to work out a smart deal of your own," she said.

"Where do you go when you leave here?" I asked.

She just smiled.

I said, "Come on, come clean, or I step over to that phone and call the police. I'm in the saddle now and I have to know."

"You going to make it tough for me?"

"If I was making it tough for you, I'd have made it tough a long time ago," I told her.

"I go to Salt Lake City. I have a daughter living there."

"Married?"

"Widowed."

"Children?"

"No, she has a little place that she keeps up. She always has room for me."

"Do you pay her anything?"

"I don't need to. She has a good job. I don't ask her for anything and she doesn't ask any questions."

"She has ideas?"

Mrs. Chester chuckled and said, "You know, she looks at me at times rather enviously. I think she thinks I'm a scarlet woman; that I'm living some kind of an immoral life."

"But she doesn't suspect what it really is?"

Mrs. Chester shook her head.

"Give me the daughter's address."

She took a piece of paper and wrote out the address.

"What's the daughter's name?"

"Eileen Adams."

"She has a telephone?"

"Yes. You want the number?"

"Put it on the memo," I said.

She said, "I'm putting myself in your power."

"*I* put you in my power," I told her. "Remember I can blow the whistle on you at any time I want to."

"You going to do it?"

"I don't know."

She looked at me wistfully. "I'm an awfully good campaigner," she said. "I know what you're after. You're smelling the money and you're going to get your fingers on it. If you'd work with me, we'd get twice as much and we could make a fair division."

"Why did you think I wanted your address?"

"So you could—Hell I don't know. Why did you?"

"I may want to work with you," I told her.

Her face lit up. "Donald," she said. "you're a good boy. You're an awfully smart boy. I knew the minute you walked into the house with that magazine racket of yours that you were awfully damned good."

"We'll let it go at that," I told her. "Be sure to keep in touch with your daughter so that I can reach you at any time. But remember one thing, I'm not making any deal with you; I'm only investigating a fraud case."

"What kind of fraud?"

"A fraudulent accident."

"There's nothing more there to investigate," she said. "You know it all already."

"I sure wish I did," I told her. "How are you coming on your ten per cent this time?"

Her face lit up again. "Donald, I'm way ahead. I'm fifteen hundred to the good right now."

"On two-bit slot machines?" I asked.

"Heavens, no," she said. "I plunge on roulette; then when my luck starts going sour, I cash in my chips and go to the dime machines. If I don't do so good there, I wait for a day and go back and try all over again. If I start perking up on the dime machines, I try the quarter machines until I've hit two or three jackpots and feel that my luck is back, and then I go to the roulette table again.

"You can't work out any kind of a mathematical system that can win at this racket because the mathematics are against you, but you can work out a rhythm system of hitting the line when you're hot and drawing in your horns when you're cold, and it pays off—believe me, Las Vegas doesn't owe me any money."

"What do you do with it?" I asked. "You got it in a bank somewhere?"

She grinned and said, "Somewhere, and that's what you can beat your brains out on, Donald. No matter what kind of threats you use, I'm not going to tell you anything about that."

"Keep it there," I told her. "Good luck to you in Las Vegas and don't go broke. Can the police get a line on your Salt Lake hideout?"

"Not a whisper of a chance," she said. "I'll use three air lines, two buses and five names getting there."

"Get started now, then," I told her, got up and walked to the door. "Want to ride the taxi back uptown?" I asked.

"Not tonight," she said. "I think my luck has had a jolt. I'm going to be hard to find."

"Okay," I told her, "I'll pay the taxi. Have luck!"

I got in the taxi and drove back to the airport.

CHAPTER TEN

I went to a Chinese restaurant and made certain that it was real Chinese, run by an old character who had a seamed face and bright, glittering eyes.

I walked up to the counter. "*Hoh shah kai mah*," I said conversationally.

That was a form of Chinese greeting, meaning "Is the whole world good?"

He was looking down at some account books he was figuring and he answered mechanically, "*Hoh shah kai.*"

Since the Chinese language is one of varying tones, it is impossible to use the rising inflection as indicative of a question. Therefore, they put the word "*mah*" on the end of a sentence to show that there is a question. By answering me, the Chinese assured me that the whole world was good.

And then suddenly he jerked his head erect in surprise as he realized that I wasn't another Chinese. "You speak Chinese?" he asked, his words all running together.'

"Just a little bit," I told him. "*Dik kom doh*. I have many Chinese friends.

"I want to write a letter to a Chinese friend. I want lots of red paper, big red envelope. Have you got one?"

I put a dollar bill on the counter.

"What kind of letter?"

"A joke letter," I said, "*gong seuh*, I need a big envelope, very very red."

He grunted, picked up the dollar, put it in the cash till, reached down under the counter and came up with a huge red envelope.

"Very fine," I said. "Now, take your brush and write in Chinese on the envelope."

"What do I write in Chinese?"

"The name of the restaurant, anything."

He hesitated a moment; then dipped the brush in the black India ink and made flowing Chinese characters down the side of the envelope.

"You read?" he asked.

I shook my head. "I don't read. I only speak a little. I have lots of Chinese friends. I learn a little from them."

"You live in Las Vegas?"

"No, Los Angeles."

I picked up the envelope and extended my hand.

He gravely shook hands with me.

I walked out; went to one of the gambling houses and looked around for advertising matter. I finally found a big piece of cardboard that would just fit in the envelope. The cardboard advertised the advantages of gambling at that particular place of business.

I put it in the envelope, sealed the envelope, went to the post office, got airmail stamps and special delivery stamps; then addressed the envelope to Clayton Dawson at the Dawson Re-Debenture Discount Security Company at Denver, Colorado, wrote the address of the office building where Helen Loomis maintained the mail drop service, and dropped the envelope in the mail.

I looked up the schedule of planes to Denver and won a little over seven hundred and fifty dollars at the crap table before I had to leave.

I rented a drive-yourself car in Denver; had a good night's sleep, and the next morning, bright and early, was where I could watch the office of Helen Loomis.

Once that red envelope with the Chinese lettering on it came in special delivery, I knew she was going to telephone her client, and I felt certain that the man who had given me the name of Clayton Dawson wasn't going to let any grass grow under his feet in finding out what was in that distinctive letter.

At nine-fifteen, a special delivery mailman delivered the mail to the Loomis office. At ten-fifteen, an attractive young woman, in a tight-fitting outfit which showed her figure to advantage, entered the office. Ten seconds later she came out carrying the big, red envelope.

She made some effort to try and keep the envelope from being quite so conspicuous, but I had chosen it with care. Outside of putting it in a brief case, she couldn't have done a thing with it where it wouldn't have stuck out like a sore thumb.

She took the elevator to the ground floor, and I was in the same cage with her.

She was exceedingly naïve, didn't pay the slightest attention to me.

I had expected a long chase by automobile, but she simply

crossed the street to the adjoining office building and went up to the seventh floor.

I hadn't intended to be so brash about it, nor had I expected to find it so easy, but since she was completely engrossed in her thoughts and apparently carrying on only a routine business errand, I got on the elevator and went up with her.

I was just a piece of animated scenery as far as she was concerned.

I had a chance to look her over as she walked down the corridor on the seventh floor. She had streamlined hips, legs that were long, straight and with just the right curves. I had the impression she was conscious of her beauty but didn't flaunt it. She went about her business quietly, competently, and the way she held her shoulders showed that she had lots of self-respect.

She was a good kid.

I followed her to an office marked *Alting L. Badger, Investments*. She opened the door and went in. I followed.

There was a receptionist at the desk with a telephone switchboard and another vacant desk.

My girl walked over the the vacant desk, picked up an office telephone, held the red envelope in front of her and started talking over the intercom.

She hung up, and a moment later a door marked "private" was pushed open with some violence and the man I had known as Clayton Dawson hurried across the office to the girl's desk, picked up the envelope, looked at it, frowned, turned it over, studied it again; then turned and started back for the private office.

"Good morning, Mr. Dawson," I said.

He whirled, looked at me, and his jaw dropped.

I said, "If you're not too busy, I'd like to have a few moments with you about that matter we were discussing."

He looked hurriedly around the office, saw the look on the faces of the two young women, said, "Very well, come in."

I followed him into a sumptuous office.

"All right," he said, "tell me, how did you do it? I suppose that envelope had something to do with it, but how in hell did you— Oh, well, it doesn't make any difference. It's done now. What's the problem?"

"The problem," I said, "is that a Los Angeles cop who is two-fisted, straight-shooting, belligerent and doesn't like glib talkers, has got his hatchet out for me. He's going to take my license."

"Why?"

"Because I tried to protect my client."

"What client?"

"You."

"So what do you want me to do?"

I said, "You seem to know all about it."

"I know a good deal about it," he said.

"I suppose Colton Essex has reported by telephone?"

"All right," he said, "suppose he has reported by telephone. Suppose I've retained him? What then?"

"I just wanted to know," I said.

"They can't touch you with a ten-foot pole," he said. "The officer knows who your client is and knows that a settlement has been made in the accident case. He'll never be able to find the victim. He'll never be able to prove you compounded a felony."

"That's not what's bothering me," I said. "Your attorney explained that very carefully and, I thought, very forcefully."

"Well, what *are* you worried about?"

"What I'm mixed in."

"You aren't mixed in anything."

"The hell I'm not," I told him. "There was a fake accident. It was all fixed up so that it would make a phony hit-and-run charge. I was to settle that, and as soon as I had made the settlement either you or your attorney tipped off Sergeant Sellers that I'd squared a hit-and-run case.

"That means that somebody knew generally of my relationship with Sergeant Sellers. It means that I was picked as a lamb for the slaughter. . . . And you can call that a pun if you want to.

"It means that I was to be put on the spot; that I was to decoy Sellers to the apartment of your so-called daughter and to the automobile she was supposed to have been driving. Then Sellers was to have the police laboratory go over that car carefully and find threads from the clothing Mrs. Chester was wearing at the time of the supposed accident.

"This would give Sellers a perfect case of hit-and-run if he could find the victim and if he could prove the accident.

"In all probablitity, he can't find the victim, and even if he does he can't prove an accident. That leaves me holding the bag. Sellers can't quite take my license, but he can hold it against me as long as I live.

"For your information, I don't like to be picked as a fall guy."

"How much do you want?" he asked.

"I want plenty."

"I'm not going to be blackmailed. I don't like blackmailers."

"I'm not talking about blackmail. I'm talking about compensation, but before I talk about that I want to know what this is all about."

"What do you mean?"

I said, "You staged a fake accident in Los Angeles. You staged it so that it would appear the woman we'll call Phyllis was driving the car; so there'd be circumstantial evidence showing that she had been driving the car.

"You know and I know that there wasn't any accident; therefore, Phyllis wasn't driving the car at the time of the accident. Therefore, the only real reason you would be so anxious to risk all this is to give yourself an alibi.

"In other words, you want to show that either you or Phyllis, or both, were in Los Angeles at the time that accident was supposed to have taken place.

"The reason you want to show that is not because you want to have it appear you were in Los Angeles, but because it is necessary for you to have it appear that you were not in Denver.

"You've taken a chance on a rap which you can beat in Los Angeles to give you an alibi on a rap which you probably can't beat in Denver.

"Now, if I work hard enough I can find out what it is. It isn't anything minor. You wouldn't have gone to all that trouble and taken all those chances unless it was something of major importance, something that involves your reputation here. Perhaps a hit-and-run while you were intoxicated; perhaps something even more serious."

"And so?" he asked.

I settled down in the chair; put my feet out in front of me and said, "And so I'm sitting right here until I know what the score is."

"You won't like it," he said.

"I know that."

"You have me where I have very little choice in the matter. I simply can't afford to have you messing around here in Denver."

"I counted on that."

"You're right," he said.

"In what?"

"That we had to have an alibi."

"Who's the we?"

"Phyllis and I. Principally Phyllis."

"Am I also right in assuming that the rap you were trying to beat here was something pretty damned serious?"

He nodded.

"What was it?" I asked.

He looked me in the eyes. "Murder," he said.

That jolted me. I came up in the chair. "Murder!"

"Yes."

"Tell me about it."

"A blackmailer," he said. "A dirty, slimy, shrewd ingenious, diabolically clever, ruthless blackmailer.

"He had compromising photographs. He had original registration cards he'd secured from hotels. He had the works."

"You couldn't deal with him?"

"He wouldn't stay put."

"So what happened?"

He sighed, started drumming on the edge of the desk. "I goofed," he said.

"In what way?"

"I wanted to get the evidence."

"What did you do?"

"I was to give him money and he was to produce the evidence."

"You met him?"

"Yes."

"Where?"

"At a little rooming house that he had selected."

"You gave him the money?"

"Yes."

"He didn't produce the evidence?"

"No, he said that he would get it for me; that he'd left it in a safe place. That he hadn't believed that I was acting in good faith. He said he had thought that I might have the police grab him and search him.

"All of that was not very smart, because if I'd wanted to go to the police, I'd have gone to them in the first place. I didn't dare to have that stuff come out. Having him searched by a police officer or anyone else was the very last thing I wanted."

"So what did you do?"

"I bought him a drink, and Phyllis put the knockout drops in it."

"Oh, oh!"

"He took the drink and right at the last realized we'd drugged him. He had a gun and tried to pull it. I clobbered him and he passed out cold. We got the keys to his apartment, his gun, and went up to his place. We searched for more than an hour before we found what we wanted. We took it. Then I went back to put the guy's keys back in his pocket."

"He was still out cold?" I asked.

"He was dead as a doornail. His heart had stopped on him."

I thought for a moment and said, "So you called Colton Essex in Los Angeles and told him you needed an absolute, ironclad alibi for yourself and Phyllis."

"Principally Phyllis," he said.

"All right, you needed an alibi for Phyllis, and you had to have it fast. You had to be be able to prove she was in Los Angeles."

"Right," he said.

I thought that over.

"Well?" he asked. "Did I do the right thing in telling you all this?"

"I asked for it. . . . Where did you get the name 'Dawson'?"

"I made it up," he said.

"Why?"

"Phyllis and I used that name and address to correspond with each other."

"You're married?"

He stroked his chin. "Yes and no."

"What do you mean by that?"

"I'm married," he said, "but my wife and I haven't been getting along for a while. She went to Las Vegas to establish a six-week's residence and get a divorce.

I raised my eyebrows. "Then why take all these chances with a blackmailer?"

"She has a damned smart lawyer," he said. "They knew that I had some outside companionship, but they couldn't prove it. She held off for nearly a year getting a divorce, trying to catch me. They had detectives shadowing me; they tried everything."

"Who's the girl in the outer office, the one who got the letter for you?"

"She's a girl I can trust."

"What's her name?"

"Mellie Belden."

"Not Millie?"

"No, Mellie."

"You trust her?"

"I trust her with my life."

"Devoted to you?"

"Devoted to the job. She's competent, capable, cool, collected and loyal."

"Helen Loomis down there knows who you are?"

"No, she knows Mellie Belden and that's all. When something comes in that's important, she telephones Mellie. She thinks Mellie is the Dawson Re-Debenture Discount Security Company."

I said, "You left a pretty wide back trail for your wife's attorney not to be able to follow it."

"They never did."

"But you were afraid they were going to?"

"If this blackmailer had gone to my wife's attorney, he could have sold the information he had for a big sum of money and he knew it."

"Who was the blackmailer?"

"Deering L. Canby."

I thought things over for a while. "How do you know he didn't?" I asked at length.

"Didn't what?"

"Go to your wife's attorney?"

"Because they didn't get the evidence. I got it."

I said, "I know a little something about blackmail and blackmailers. When there's a competitive market they like to sell to the highest bidder."

"This one didn't," Badger said.

I thought some more. "You agreed on a price?"

"Yes."

"How much?"

"Twenty thousand."

"It was worth more?"

"I'd have paid a hundred if I'd had to."

"You met him at this rooming house?"

"Yes."

"He picked it?"

"Yes. He said he wanted to be certain the room wasn't bugged."

"But he didn't have the stuff you wanted with him?"

"No."

"Was a specific time fixed?"

He said, "Why do you ask that?"

"It might be important."

"A very specific time was fixed and he warned me not to be over two minutes late."

"Late?"

"That's right."

"You could have been earlier than the appointed time and that

69

would have been all right, but you couldn't be over two minutes late?"

"That's right."

I thought some more.

"How long before you'll be in the clear on your divorce?" I asked at length.

"About ten days now."

I took a long breath. "You had me mixed up in a hit-and-run deal," I said, "and now I've listened to you and I'm mixed in a murder case up to my necktie. Some things are confidential, but information on a murder isn't. If I don't go to the police with this, I'll be in a jam."

He spread out his hands, palms upward. "You left me with no choice in the matter. I had to tell you. You were hot on the trail, and you'd have found it out."

"Yes," I said, "I'd have found it out. I intended to cover the police blotter for the time you had built your alibi and check on every crime . . . What do the police know about Deering Canby?"

"They know he was a blackmailer; they know that he was keeping an appointment with someone he was blackmailing; they know he had knockout drops slipped in his drink and that he was killed and they think papers and evidence were taken from his body.

"They know that Phyllis' car was parked in the neighborhood. That's why we had to work fast. They're looking for her to question her and when they find her she has to have an alibi.

"I want the police in Los Angeles to give her her alibi before things get too hot up here."

I was silent for a while.

"Well?" he asked. "You going to blow the whistle?"

"I don't know," I said.

"If you don't," he told me, "you can write your own ticket."

"How strong?"

"The sky's the limit. This means a lot to me now. They've been talking about running me for mayor. I'm a prominent citizen here. This scandal would break me wide open. The information in the hands of my wife would cost me a cool half a million."

"Where did you get the idea for the knockout drops?" I asked.

"My wife," he said. "She'd been a nurse before I married her."

"She told you about chloral hydrate?"

"Yes."

"That stuff is dangerous," I said.

"I know it now. A great deal depends upon the condition of a man's system, his heart, and all that—but we gave the guy what we thought was only enough to knock him out for half an hour. We had a long search in his apartment. I was afraid he was going to come to and make a squawk before we could get out."

"Where did this take place?"

"At the Round Robin Rooms. He wanted to pick the place because he wanted to be sure it wasn't bugged. He rented the room."

"You and I have a good deal in common," I told him.

He raised his eyebrows.

"We're both in one hell of a mess," I said. "I'll contact you later."

He reached for his wallet. "You want money?"

"Not now," I told him. "Later."

I left the office and walked to my hotel, thinking the thing over.

I stopped at the desk and got the key to my room.

A man stepped forward and said, "Donald Lam?"

I looked at him and nodded.

"Okay," he said, "I've got a warrant for you from Los Angeles, compounding a felony, squaring a hit-and-run. You want to waive extradition?"

I said, "I'll send a telegram and tell you then."

He said, "We were told we'd have trouble."

"Not with me," I told him. "I'm docile as a kitten."

I sent a telegram to Colton C. Essex, attorney at law:

ARRESTED IN DENVER COLORADO FOR COMPOUNDING FELONY AND SQUARING HIT AND RUN. AM AT PRESENT IN CUSTODY OF DENVER POLICE. SHALL I WAIVE EXTRADITION.

I signed it *Donald Lam*, and turned to the plain-clothes officer, "Okay," I said, "let's go."

CHAPTER ELEVEN

They put me in a cell in the Denver jail. After an hour, a trusty came with a telegram for me. The telegram had been opened, read, stamped, censored and was handed to me in that condition.

The telegram was signed by Colton C. Essex. It said,

WIRE RECEIVED. SIT TIGHT. AT THE PROPER REPEAT PROPER TIME EVERYTHING WILL BE UNDERTAKEN TO BRING YOUR CASE TO SATIS-FACTORY CONCLUSION. SIT TIGHT. SAY NOTHING. KEEP COOL.

I asked if I had the priviledge of sending out for a meal which I could pay for out of my own pocket and was advised I didn't have that privilege.

I asked about bail. I was told that would be arranged in due time, but if I wanted to sign a paper waiving extradition, I could have quite a few courtesies.

I said I was sitting tight.

I was told that a man was due to arrive to take me back to Los Angeles to face the charges in California. Again, I was told I would make it a lot easier for myself if I waived extradition.

I had a poor night.

Frank Sellers was there in the morning.

They took me from the cell up to an office where a couple of plainclothes men sat at a table, and Frank Sellers spoke in such carefully guarded language that I knew the room was bugged and everything I said was being taped.

"Well, Pint Size," Sellers said, "you didn't do so good. Want to tell us about it?"

"Tell you about what?"

"About the whole thing."

"I have nothing to tell."

"I'm in a little different position now than when I was talking with you the last time," he said. "Now I've got a witness that saw the woman being struck by the automobile."

"Did he get the license number?" I asked.

"We don't need the license number," Sellers said. "We got the car. We've got a perfect case of circumstantial evidence."

"How come?"

"Fibers from the fabric of the skirt the woman was wearing were found adhering to the undercarriage of the automobile. It's a perfect match."

Sellers turned to one of the detectives and said conversationally "That's a Colorado license plate on the number. We've got the owner all right, Phyllis Eldon, who resides here in Denver."

One of the detectives nodded; then suddenly stiffened to attention. "Wait a minute," he said, "did you say Eldon, E-L-D-O-N?"

"That's right."

"When was this accident? This hit-and-run you're talking about?"

Sellers looked at his notebook. "On the twenty-first," he said.

"What time on the twenty-first?"

"Eight o'clock in the evening."

Both Denver detectives were sitting straight up at attention.

One of them said, "Wait a minute, this Eldon dame is one we've been wanting to question in connection with . . ." He suddenly broke off and looked at me.

"Well, she's in L. A.," Sellers said. "I've got her spotted. All I need to make a perfect case is to find out what Pint Size here has done with the victim. He made a pay-off and has her under cover."

"Wait a minute—wait a minute," one of the Denver detectives said, "let's not do any more talking right now. Take him back to his cell."

"There's no use taking him back now and letting him think it over," Sellers said. "I'm putting it on the line with him. He is in bad. I offered him a deal if he'd give us the information. He told us who his client was. It's a phony. He's been double-crossing me. His license is on the line right now and he's in bad. We've got a charge against him, compounding a felony."

The detective leaned toward Sellers. "We've got a little talking to do," he said. "We don't want him in on it." He turned to me and said, "Come on, Lam, come with me."

Sellers started to protest but was outnumbered. He looked mad and puzzled as they beckoned to me.

I followed the detective back down the corridor, was delivered to a turnkey and escorted back to my cell.

I stayed there.

CHAPTER TWELVE

I was kept out of circulation for two hours, then I was brought back to a meeting that had evidently been far from harmonious.

The two Denver police officers were there; a deputy district attorney was there; Sergeant Sellers was there; and Colton C. Essex, the attorney, was there.

Essex jumped up to greet me with a cordial handshake. "Well, well, Lam, how are you?" he said. "I got here just as soon as I could. I had to charter planes. This is an outrage."

"I'm doing all right," I said.

He squeezed my hand hard. "I'm representing you," he said, "and *I'll do the talking*."

"You've done enough of it already," Sellers said.

"Well, gentlemen," Essex said, turning around and putting a protective hand on my shoulder, "this man is probably in a position to bring suit for false arrest, but he's not vindictive. However, if he isn't released immediately, I'm going to file habeas corpus."

Sellers said, "I tell you the guy squared a hit-and-run charge."

"What hit-and-run charge?"

"You know damned well what hit-and-run charge!" Sellers said.

"I'm beginning to think this may have been a frameup, this whole business," Essex said. "Somebody certainly has it in for my client, Phyllis Eldon. You can see for yourselves, gentlemen, these Denver detectives swear they have a witness, whose name they're not prepared to disclose, who saw her automobile here in Denver, Colorado, at the time of the Canby death—a death which the authorities here believe is a murder.

"On the other hand, Sergeant Sellers says he has two witnesses who definitely swear that automobile was in Los Angeles within an interval of four hours."

"Now, wait a minute," Sellers said. "They don't identify that automobile."

"I thought you just said they did."

74

"Well, I say that that's the automobile that struck down this Mrs. Chester."

"No one got the license number?"

"Well, they got the time of the accident. They saw her hit and we know what automobile did the hitting. We've got perfect circumstantial evidence that would result in a conviction in front of any jury in the world."

"Providing you had a complaining witness," Essex said.

Sellers turned to glower at me. "Thanks to this little pint-sized bastard," he said, "we've got no complaining witness at the moment, but we're going to get her.

"When we get her and she tells her story, it's just going to be too bad for Pint Size, here."

"My client's name," Essex said, with dignity, "is Donald Lam. If you expect any courtesies in connection with failure to file suit for malicious prosecution and unlawful arrest, you had better be a little more courteous in turn.

Sellers clamped down on his cigar so hard that I thought he was going to bite it in two.

"Well, we don't seem to be getting anyplace," the deputy district attorney said. "If Mr. Lam intends to file application for a writ of habeas corpus and the evidence isn't any stronger than it appears at the present time, I would suggest this man be turned loose."

"The evidence isn't strong because he's damned well seen to it that the key evidence is missing," Sellers said.

"Well," the deputy district attorney assured him, "as soon as you've established that point by proper evidence, Sergeant, you will have redress against him in California."

"You're damned right I'll have redress against him in California."

"Under the circumstances," Essex said, "I see no reason why my client should be longer detained."

He got up, nodded to me and said, "Come on, Lam."

I got up and followed him to the door. As I walked past Sellers I thought he was going to grab me and physically restrain me, but he controlled himself, sitting there glowering and chomping on the soggy cigar butt.

We walked out.

"How did you get here?" I asked Essex.

"Chartered planes."

I said, "Somebody must be putting up money in this case."

"Your assumption," he said, "is certainly logical."

"Lots of money," I went on.

"I wouldn't get in this position otherwise."

"You're representing me?"

He said, "Let's get in the car before I answer that question."

He led the way to his rented car; then he rolled up the windows, turned to me and said, "Yes, I'm representing you just as long as you continue to be loyal to your clients."

"I know who those clients are now," I said.

"I understand you do."

"Where's Mrs. Chester?" I said. "If they find her, it's going to be—"

"For your private, confidential information," he said, "Mrs. Chester is due to land in Mexico City at six o'clock tomorrow morning. Within three hours of the time she lands, she's going to be at an isolated resort in the country."

"Will she stay put?" I asked.

"Long enough."

"Who's the mysterious witness that is trying to put Phyllis' automobile in Denver four hours before the accident in Los Angeles?"

He regarded me searchingly for a long time. Then he said, "Lam, my client tells me you know enough so I am going to take you entirely into my confidence."

"That's always advisable," I told him.

He said, "The person who is making all the trouble in this case, as you probably realize, is Mrs. Alting L. Badger."

"And why is she making all this trouble?"

"Because," he said, "she wants a settlement of two million five hundred thousand dollars."

"How much is she going to get?"

"One hundred and fifty thousand."

"Is Badger that well fixed?" I asked.

He smiled and said, "I'm not prepared to discuss my client's exact worth; but, as a man who knows his way around, you can see the risks I'm taking in this case, and I can assure you that I am not a cheap attorney."

"All right," I said, "while we're putting it on the line, I'm taking risks and, if I play ball, I'm not going to be a cheap detective."

"Nobody wants you to."

"What's your definition of cheap?" I asked.

"What's yours?"

I said, "I'd expect quite a bonus."

He looked at me. "Look. Lam, you're supposed to be brainy. I think you are. You've played your cards pretty smooth. If you can squeeze us out of this one, you can just about name your own figure."

"But I have to keep quiet?"

"Hell," he said, "you have to keep quiet for your own sake. What's going to happen if Sergeant Sellers gets hold of Mrs. Harvey W. Chester?"

"All she can say is that I told her I had a client that wanted to buy up the claim that she had against some unknown driver."

"That would have worked all right at the time," he said, "but your subsequent actions in locating the identity of the various interested parties would look like hell in front of a jury."

I thought that over.

"Particularly with Sellers manipulating the evidence and offering Mrs. Chester complete immunity if she'd give testimony that would result in your conviction and in forfeiting your license."

"I can see your point," I said.

"All right," he told me, "you're going to the airport and get out of Colorado as quickly as possible."

"California?" I asked, raising my eyebrows.

"Hell, no," he said. "California is bad business for you at the present time. Here's a credit card made out in your name. Go to Las Vegas; get anything you want, including a reasonable supply of cash for gambling so you don't get bored. Telephone my office and tell my secretary where you are. You don't need to tell her any names, just say, 'Tell Mr. Essex that I'm at such-and-such an address.'"

"What about my partner, Bertha Cool?"

Essex was thoughtful. "Your partner, Mrs. Cool, is, I understand, in a rather hostile mood. I think it might be better not to let her know where you could be reached."

I said, "My confidential secretary is Elsie Brand. She's been with me for a long time and you can trust her all the way. After I communicate with you, see that she knows where I am."

"She won't communicate with Mrs. Cool?" he asked.

"Hell, no!" I said.

"All right," he told me, "I think we'd better get to the airport. You only have half an hour before your plane leaves."

77

CHAPTER THIRTEEN

I got aboard the plane among the first passengers and seated myself next to a window.

A woman seated herself next to me.

I didn't think much of it at the time, but after I fastened my seat belt and looked around, I noticed that there were still quite a few vacant window seats. It was a flight where seats had not been assigned and, things being what they were, I gave my seat companion a sidelong glance.

She was somewhere around thirty-five to forty, and she'd spent lots of money trying to look five years younger than she was. She was as well groomed as soft leather, but there was a certain hardness about her that showed through the grooming.

I wondered if Sellers had planted a stooge.

I surreptitiously looked her over a second time and decided she wasn't a policewoman, and no private detective could afford to dress like that, so I decided she had some particular reason for wanting that seat and stretched out and relaxed.

The plane gunned into action, took off down the runway, hesitated for a few seconds, then roared into speed.

My woman companion closed her eyes.

The plane lifted off the ground, zoomed sharply upward; then the pilot throttled the motors down.

She said, "I'm always nervous during take-off."

I knew then that it wasn't an accident, so I smiled a vague smile and wondered if someone was going to pick up my trail at Las Vegas and if I'd be shadowed twenty-four hours a day.

Ordinarily, police aren't in a position to do that kind of shadowing except on the most important cases, and unless Sellers had tapped a till, he didn't have money enough to keep me under that kind of surveillance.

I checked my impressions by playing hard to get—not upstage, particularly, but preoccupied with my thoughts.

I felt her eyes on my profile.

After a moment, she said, "You have the most interesting hands I've seen in a long time—I hope you don't think me forward."

"What about my hands?" I asked.

She laughed and said, "I'm one of those women who tell fortunes—not professionally, of course, just as private readings for my close friends. . . . The hands show character."

"What about *my* hands?" I asked.

She gently reached over, picked up my right hand, spread it out on her lap and caressed the fingers.

"You have imagination," she said, "a great deal of ingenuity. You use applied imagination in your work, whatever your work is.

"There are several women in your life, but you keep them at a distance. There's an older woman with whom you have some sort of a business relationship and whom you irritate tremendously, and there's a younger woman who is eating her heart out for you. She has been in love with you for a long time.

"You're in some sort of a profession where it's hard to be married and you're too much of a gentleman to just take advantage of this girl."

She raised her eyes to mine and looked at me steadily.

Her eyes were green and it seemed the pupils were abnormally small.

"You understand?" she asked.

"You're doing the talking," I told her.

She laughed, a hard metallic laugh. "Now, don't challenge me," she said, "because when people are difficult that way I usually jar them right down to their shoe tops."

"How?" I asked.

"By telling them things that they think I couldn't possibly know."

"Isn't all fortune telling like that?" I asked.

"Well, mostly what I do is character reading, and, of course, character shapes environment."

"You sound very interesting," I said, looking at her as though I had really started seeing her for the first time. "What are you, a writer?"

"No," she laughed.

"What?" I asked.

She hesitated provocatively, then said, "No, I'm not going to tell you now. What's *your* name?"

"Lam," I said, "Donald Lam."

She said, "Call me Minny—short for Minerva."

"And the last name?"

She placed her extended forefinger on her lips, glanced at me archly, and said, "Isn't Minny enough?"

79

I smiled and said, "It's always the woman who tells the man where to stop.'

"I'll bet they don't tell you to stop very often, Donald."

"Is that guesswork or character reading?"

"Well," she said, "it's a general observation. Let's get back to your hand."

She opened the hand wide, stretched the fingers, gently stroked them with her hand, said, "It's a wonderful hand, Donald. You are something of a genius. You are engaged in some peculiar occupation, something mysterious about it. . . . Tell me, Donald, are you in the secret service or with the F.B.I.?"

"If I were in the secret service," I said, "do you think I would admit it?"

"I don't know. Are you supposed to keep it secret?"

"I don't know, am I?"

She laughed and said, "You're being very, very cagey—you're also in trouble of some sort, Donald. Someone is trying to make trouble for you. Someone who is very powerful—you're going to have to be careful. You're going to have to be very careful."

I jerked my hand away and closed the fingers.

She looked at me and smiled. "I told you I'd jar you right down to your boot tops, Donald. I hit it right, didn't I?"

"Yes," I said curtly.

"You want to tell me about it?"

"No."

"Lots of times people tell me about their troubles," she said, "and I'm able to help them."

"How do you help them?"

"Some sort of an extrasensory perception, I guess."

I hesitated a moment, then said, "No, I can't tell you. It would be violating a confidence."

"A professional confidence?"

"In a way."

"Donald, are you a lawyer?"

"No."

She regarded me thoughtfully, said, "You've been traveling lately. There's something in Los Angeles that's bothering you."

I didn't say anything.

"Something in connection with a man and a woman—some surreptitious relationship. You know something that—well, that's as far as I can go."

"Why?"

"Because when I said that, you interposed a shield between

your mind and mine. I guess perhaps I've tried to help you too much, Donald. I was interested in you when I saw your hands, but if you don't want help, that's all right.

"I can tell you this much, however, you're going into a period of great danger. People whom you think are entirely on your side are using you, Donald. They're using you deliberately and selfishly and when they get done they're going to cast you to one side. They'll throw you to the wolves.

"Please, Donald, please don't trust everybody the way you do. You're riding for a fall if you don't start looking out for number one."

"Thank you," I said.

"Donald, you've still done it."]

"Done what?"

"Kept that shield between us. I can't get that flow of thought any more."

"You do have a lot of extrasensory perception, don't you?" I said.

"I think I do, Donald. I'm going to stop bothering you now, because I can see that I've disturbed you and, in the position that you're in right at the moment, you can't afford to be disturbed. You've got to have your emotional reflexes all clear so that you can think with chain-lightning rapidity—only, do this one thing for me, please, think for yourself. Think of what's going to happen or what may happen before you put yourself in anyone else's power.

"You've got your head in a lion's mouth now, and I can tell you frankly the lion firmly intends to bite that head off as soon as you have served his purpose.

"How far are you going, Donald, all the way to Los Angeles?"

"No, I'm getting off at Las Vegas."

"Are you?" she said. "I'm getting off at Las Vegas, too."

"You live there?"

Abruptly, she put her hand in my lap. "Take a look," she said.

"At what?"

"I told you everything from looking at your hand. If you want to find out anything about me, you'll have to tell me from looking at my hand."

She laughed.

The stewardess walked by, and Minny smiled at her and said, "May I have a magazine, please?"

"Any particular one that you wanted?"

"Just let me see what you have, please."

The stewardess brought her some magazines. She selected both *Look* and *Life*, thumbed through the pages, completely absorbed in the pictures and printed matter.

I sat rigidly erect looking out of the window.

After about thirty minutes, she closed the magazines, said abruptly, "I jarred you, didn't I, Donald?"

"Yes," I said.

"And you've still got that mental shield up."

"I have to keep it up."

She said, "Be particularly cautious about someone who's paying you money to do something for him, but who is preparing to double-cross you—and a lawyer enters into it somewhere. I can't get the whole sketch right now, but people that you think are your friends are getting ready to give you the double cross. You're going to have to be very, very careful, Donald, because they have you in such a position that almost everything you do is playing directly into their hands."

I let myself nod almost imperceptibly.

Abruptly, she folded the magazines, said, "I won't bother you any more, Donald. I'm going to sleep."

She settled back and closed her eyes.

We got to the point where the stewardess announced that we were starting to descend for Las Vegas, and that passengers would please observe the sign about fastening seat belts, and later on, the No Smoking sign.

Minny opened her eyes, fastened her seat belt, smiled at me; then closed her eyes again.

We glided into a smooth landing, and Minny got to her feet the minute the plane had come to a stop. Using her feminine prerogative, she pushed forward and was out of the plane sometime before I was able to get to the ground.

I looked round and failed to see her.

I went over to the rack where incoming baggage was placed and saw no trace of her.

She had vanished into thin air.

All that was left was the warning in my ears.

I went to the telegraph office and wired Colton C. Essex at his office in Los Angeles:

SEND ME DESCRIPTION AND ADDRESS OF MINERVA BADGER CARE WESTERN UNION IN LAS VEGAS.

I signed it *Donald Lam* and went to a hotel.

CHAPTER FOURTEEN

At the hotel, I climbed into a bathtub and tried to scrub off the sickly sweet smell of jail disinfectant.

I knew that most of the odor was still in my nose rather than on my body, but I gave my body a good scrubbing anyway.

I went to a restaurant, had a good meal, a good night's sleep, and about noon stopped by the Western Union office.

A telegram had just come in for me. It read:

ARE YOU CRAZY. DON'T GO NEAR THAT WOMAN. AGE 37, GREEN EYES, MEDIUM BUILD, HAIR CURRENTLY CHESTNUT. WEIGHT 115 LBS. DANGEROUS AS A RATTLESNAKE. ADDRESS, COOKINETTE APARTMENTS, LAS VEGAS, FIVE WEEKS OF JURISDICTIONAL RESIDENCE COMPLETE. REPORTEDLY HAS BEEN HIRING PRIVATE DETECTIVES. GIVE HER A WIDE BERTH. THIS IS IMPERATIVE.

The telegram was signed *Essex*.

I sent him a telegram in reply.

AM NOT CRAZY. PARTY HAS ASSUMED THE INITIATIVE. APPARENTLY SMELLS A VERY LARGE RAT.

I signed it *Donald*.

I did a little gambling, killed a little time, and put through a person-to-person call to Elsie Brand at the office.

"How are you coming, Elsie?" I asked.

"I was ready just to close the desk and go home," she said. "Where are you, Donald?"

"It's probably better if you don't know," I said. "How are things at the office?"

"Tight. Very, very tight."

"Got any money?"

"I can get some."

"Get on a plane that reaches Las Vegas at ten-thirty tonight. I'll meet you."

"Oh, Donald, I can't make it."

"Sure you can."

"Well, I'll . . . I'll try. What do I tell Bertha?"

"Tell her nothing. Leave a note that you won't be in tomorrow."

"Donald, Bertha is fit to be tied."

"Let's tie her then."

She laughed nervously. "I'll be on the plane," she said.

"Bring a brief case, notebooks, pencils and that small tape recorder, the one that works with flashlight batteries. We may need it."

"Donald, Bertha told me if I heard from you at all or knew where you were, I was to let her know at once."

"She's in touch with Sellers?"

"He's been in the office two or three times."

"How does he feel?"

"Chewing cigars like mad, pacing the floor and telling Bertha she's got to bail out before everything crashes."

"And Bertha wants to bail out?" I asked.

"I don't know, Donald. She got mad at Sellers the last time he was in and told him that she wasn't going to condemn you without a hearing. He got mad at her and told her he'd been jeopardizing his standing on the force, trying to protect her on account of friendship, and that she couldn't presume on it too far."

"That's fine," I told her. "Keep the pot boiling."

"Well, don't you think for a minute it isn't boiling—Are you going to meet me at the plane, Donald?"

"Yes."

"Donald, have you got . . . accommodations?"

"Yes."

"One room or two?" she asked.

"Two."

"Oh."

She was silent for a while.

"You'll be there?"

"I'll be there."

"Okay, I'll meet you."

I hung up and went down to the telegraph office.

Essex was burning up the wires:

SMELLING A RAT AND CATCHING A RAT ARE TWO DIFFERENT THINGS. KEEP AWAY FROM THE TRAP AND I MEAN FAR AWAY.

I sent him a wire: "I'M NOT A RAT."

And signed it *Donald*.

Then I had a session at the tables, dinner, drove around enough to shake shadows, then went to a motel, looked the place over and selected two adjoining units which had a connecting door.

After I had registered and paid in advance, I went to the airport and picked up Elsie as she got off the plane.

She was starry-eyed with excitement. Her fingers dug into my arm. "Oh, Donald, this is *so* exciting! You have something for me to do—I mean, this is business?"

"Business," I said.

"You really have *two* rooms?"

"I wouldn't lie to you. But there's a connecting door."

She didn't say anything for a while.

We got her baggage, got in the car I had rented, and I drove her to the motel. I felt it might be a good plan to keep moving around and, with a rented car and a motel while still retaining my room at the hotel, I was in a little more flexible position.

"You left a note for Bertha?" I asked her.

"Yes, I just left a note and said I wouldn't be in. You know what that means, she'll probably fire me."

"She can't fire you," I said. "You're *my* secretary. She can fire her own secretary if she wants to, but she can't fire you. We've been through that before. You're mine."

She started to say something, then lowered her eyes demurely. "Yes," she said, and then, after a moment added, "I am."

CHAPTER FIFTEEN

After I was satisfied I hadn't been followed, I moved Elsie Brand's bag from the car into her room at the motel.

She looked it over and said, "Where's the connecting door, Donald?"

I showed her.

"It goes into your room?"

I nodded, opened the door, and we went through.

She started to say something, then blushed and checked herself.

"Now listen, Elsie," I told her, "this is going to be quite an assignment. I want you to get it straight. You see this closet door?"

She nodded.

"At the top there's a metal latticework," I said. "That's to give the closet ventilation. There's no window in the closet. It's a big closet."

She looked at me inquiringly.

I said, "I have a room in a downtown hotel here. I think that when I go back to that room a shadow will pick me up and an attempt will be made to follow me wherever I go from that point on.

"I'm going to drive directly back here to this motel, pretending that I'm naïve enough not to worry about being followed."

"You think you *will* be followed?"

"I'm almost certain of it."

"But Donald, if you got this place as a hideout, why do you lead people directly to it?"

"Because I'm ready to lead people to it now," I told her.

"I'm afraid I don't understand."

I said, "I come back to the motel. We leave the door to the connecting room wide open until I come in."

She lowered her eyes.

"If anyone knocks on my door," I said, "you take your notebook, hurry into that closet as fast as you can, closing the connecting door behind you, and also the closet door. In the closet you can hear what's being said. You take down the conversation in shorthand as far as possible but we'll fix up this tape recorder now so the microphone is just underneath this metal grille. Everything that's said in the room will be registered on the tape.

"You will of course have to be very, very silent. If anyone suspects you're in there—well it *could* be dangerous."

"Donald," she said, "I'll be all right, but you'll be in danger."

I said, "I think things are going to be all right. Are you game to try it?"

"Of course I am. I'll do anything, Donald, anything—for you."

"Good girl," I told her. "Now it's late. You get everything settled, rig up that tape recorder. You know how to do it. Tie the microphone to the grille, have things all fixed up by the time I get back. I'll be gone about thirty minutes. I'm going to go to my hotel, go out, drive around the block, then make a beeline for this place."

"And you feel sure you'll be followed?"

"I'm almost certain I'll be followed."

"How long will it be after you get back before someone knocks on the door?"

"Probably only a minute or two."

"All right," she said. "I think I'd better move into the closet within about twenty minutes."

"Good girl," I told her, and patted her on the shoulder. "I'm on my way."

I drove the rented car to a parking place at the hotel, got my key, went up to my room, fooled around for a minute or two, then came back looking over my shoulder once or twice, got into the car, drove around the block, and then made a beeline back to the motel.

I opened the door of my room and walked in.

The connecting door was closed. I looked in the closet.

Elsie had the tape recorder all set up on a chair and she was seated in another chair, her open notebook on her lap and pencils arranged on a chair.

"Good girl," I said.

She blew me a kiss.

There was a knock at the outer door.

I hurriedly closed the closet door, went to the outer door, opened it and then fell back in surprise.

The woman who was standing there wasn't the one I had expected.

"Hello, Donald," she said.

"Good Lord," I said, "what are *you* doing here?"

Mrs. Chester said, "I kept thinking about the smell of that

money, Donald. You know I just *couldn't* get it out of my mind. I'm not young any more and my racket is getting pretty much worn out."

I said, "You were supposed to—"

"Yes, I know," she said smiling. "I was supposed to go to Mexico City and then I was to be picked up and taken out in the country someplace where no one would ever find me, and it's not nice to double-cross people, is it, Donald?"

"I wouldn't know," I said.

"I never like to do it," she admitted, "but there *are* times when one has to. After all, self-preservation is the first law of nature, you know."

She had moved quietly and unobtrusively into the room while she was talking and now I closed the door.

I said, "You're hotter than a stove lid. Sergeant Sellers has got thirty detectives working on your trail. If you stay here, he'll find you just as sure as shooting."

She smiled at me and said, "You wouldn't like that, would you, Donald?"

I thought my answer over carefully. I said, "It means nothing to me but apparently there are people who wouldn't like it. And I don't think you're going to like it very well because they'd put you in a spot."

"I am in a spot," she said. "I know it."

She sat down and smiled at me.

"Also," she went on, "I know that you're in a spot, Donald, and I know that the people who are back of you would be very much inconvenienced if the police should find me. Therefore it's up to you and up to those people to see that the police don't find me."

"They'll find you anywhere in this country," I said.

"Not if you hide me, Donald. You've got brains."

"And you want me to hide you?"

She said, "I want you to hide me from the police, that's all. I want to be in contact with you. I'm using this nose of mine. It's an educated nose, Donald. It smells money trails just like a bloodhound can smell where people have left a trail."

"What do you want?"

"I want to go to Mexico but I want money first."

"How much money?"

She smiled at me and said, "All I can get, Donald. You should know that."

"And how much do you think you can get?"

She said, "I got ten thousand. I was to keep five. I gave five of it back. I shouldn't have done that."

"Why?"

"I should have held onto that five and asked for twenty-five more. I think I'd have got it."

I said, "What you're doing amounts to blackmail."

She smiled affably and said, "It does, doesn't it, Donald?"

"Yes, it does, and that could be serious," I said.

"Everything in life can be serious, but you have to gamble once in a while."

I said, "You were given money to go to Mexico City?"

"That's right."

"You know who gave you the money?"

"Of course, Donald, whenever anyone gives me money I know who it is."

I said, "You'd better get in touch with that person and tell him you want more money. Don't tell me. I can't do anything about it."

"I think you can, Donald," she said. "I think you can do it better than I can. I think you can present my case to better advantage. My nose smells money, but you're the one to get it."

"How did you know I was here?"

"Bless your heart, I followed you from the hotel. That's a pretty slick idea to have a room in a hotel and then go out to a motel someplace to sleep—but you shouldn't have been so obvious about it, Donald. I'm not a very good driver but I followed you just as easy as could be. I didn't have any trouble at all."

I mopped my forehead with a handkerchief.

There was a knock at the door.

Mrs. Chester looked at me in dismay. "Were you expecting somebody—at this hour?"

I said, "You called, and if you called, somebody else could."

She said, "I could hide somewhere. How about in that closet?"

I shook my head. "I'm not hiding you. This may be the police for all I know. They're looking everywhere for you, Mrs. Chester."

She said, "Remember, Donald, when I smell money I have to keep sniffing. That's my nature."

I strode over and opened the door.

The woman who had been seated next to me on the plane was standing there with a smile.

"Hello, Donald," she said seductively, and moved on into the room, then stopped as she saw Mrs. Chester standing with one hand on the door leading to the bathroom.

"Well, well, well," she said. "What's this?"

I said, "May I ask what you're doing here? More fortune-telling?"

"More fortunetelling, Donald," she said. "I got worried about you and I thought that perhaps it was time you and I had a nice long talk—but *who* is *this* woman?"

"She is a woman I barely know," I said. "She dropped in wanting something and I've already given her the advice she wants."

I nodded to the door.

"Thank you," Mrs. Chester said, and started out.

Mrs. Badger moved between her and the door, "*Just* a minute," she said.

Mrs. Chester stopped and looked at her and then looked at me.

Mrs. Badger's eyes narrowed. "Oh, oh," she said, "I'm beginning to get a picture, a very, very beautiful picture."

There was a tense silence in the room.

I said, "You may jump to a lot of false conclusions, Mrs. . . . Minny."

She looked at me and said, "You *are* smart, aren't you?"

I said nothing.

She said, "You started to call me by my right name. I should have known you'd run me to earth in time. But, by the same token, Donald, I think I hold a few trump cards myself. In fact, I think I've got enough trumps now to make a grand slam."

She said almost musically, "This officer from Los Angeles was after you because you'd hidden a woman who was mixed up in a hit-and-run suit. You wouldn't tell him where she was. You said you didn't know.

"Now, I heard just enough while I was listening outside the door to let me know that I'm getting in on something pretty juicy. I think that I'm going to get my hooks into something I've always wanted."

She turned to Mrs. Chester and said, "I believe he called you Mrs. Chester."

Mrs. Chester glanced at me helplessly.

"And," Minny went on, "you wanted money. You said your nose could smell money. Well, dearie, if you've got a good nose and can smell money, you just come right along with me, because you and I are going to do some smelling together."

Mrs. Chester's face lit up. "You aren't turning me over to the cops?"

Minny laughed and said, "You're my ace in the hole, dearie.

That nose of yours has finally smelled the way to money, lots of money."

"You've got it?" Mrs. Chester asked.

"I'm going to get it," Minny said. "You and I are going to get it together."

"I'm afraid I don't understand," Mrs. Chester said.

"Bless your soul, you don't have to. You just need to tell me the whole story, just put your cards on the table," Mrs. Badger said. "When you finish talking, I'll pick the trumps and start trumping everything in sight. Then we'll have money, lots of money."

"Twenty thousand dollars?" Mrs. Chester asked.

Minny laughed. "A hundred thousand for your share if you do *exactly* as I tell you."

Mrs. Chester's face lit into a beatific smile. "Darling," she said, "I had a feeling of panic when you walked in, and then right away this nose of mine began to twitch. I think we're on the right track now. Where do we go?"

"Where we can talk," Minny said, "and where you can meet with my attorney."

"Is he a good lawyer?" Mrs. Chester asked.

"The best."

"Can he keep me out of trouble in Los Angeles?"

Minny laughed and said, "You're in Nevada now. This attorney of mine has all the political pull in the world. If you don't waive extradition, you can stay in Nevada as long as you live, provided you haven't committed a murder in California."

"It wasn't a murder," Mrs. Chester said. "It was . . . well, sort of a fraud."

Minny laughed. "Come on, dearie," she said. "I want you to meet a *good* lawyer and then we'll do a little talking."

She held the door open and smiled at me. "Goodnight, Donald," she said.

The door slammed.

The closet door opened. Elsie, looking white and frightened, came out and said, "Is that what you expected?"

"That," I told her, "was *not* what I expected."

"What we do now?" Elsie asked.

"Now," I said, "you go into that bedroom, take the tape recorder and your notebook, lock the connecting door, and go to bed. Don't open up either the connecting door or your outside door for anything or anyone other than me, and make absolutely certain I'm the one at the door before you open."

"Where are you going, Donald?"

"I'm going out and start picking up pieces," I said.

"Pieces?" she asked.

"The shattered pieces of my career, Elsie."

She came to me then and put her arms around me. "Donald, is it serious?"

"It's so damned serious that I don't like to think about it," I said. "Sergeant Sellers has probably got what he wants. I've botched up a case and, taken by and large, there's going to be hell to pay."

She stood on her tiptoes then to kiss me. "Donald," she said, after a moment, "remember that you have me and my faith in you. We'll come out on top of the heap yet."

"Well, we're sure at the bottom now," I told her. "But thanks for your support."

This time I kissed her. It was a long, lingering kiss.

"Do you have to go, Donald?" she asked.

"That," I told her, "is the understatement of the week. I have to go now and I have to go fast."

She stood watching me wistfully as I dashed out of the door, slamming it behind me.

CHAPTER SIXTEEN

From the nearest public phone booth I called the night number Essex had given me.

His voice sounded sleepy.

"Wake up," I said. "The fat's in the fire."

"What do you mean?"

I said, "Minerva is on the warpath. She's grabbed every trump in the deck."

"Damn it, Lam," he said, irritably, "I told you to keep away from her and—"

"I kept away from her," I said. "She was the one who picked up my trail and ran *me* down."

"Well, you don't have to talk to her."

"It isn't anything I'll say," I told him. "It's what Mrs. Chester's saying."

"What Mrs. . . . *WHO*? *Who* did you say?"

"I said Mrs. Chester."

"She's in Mexico."

"That's what you think. She came to try and blackmail me, and Minny moved in on the deal."

"Where is Mrs. Chester now?"

"Talking with Minerva Badger and Minerva Badger's attorney," I said.

"Oh, my God," he said, in a voice that was almost a wail. Then after a moment, he said, "That's the end of the line, we're ruined."

"You give up?" I asked.

"If she's got Mrs. Chester," Essex said, "we might just as well throw in the towel."

"All right," I told him, "call up your client, tell him to get under cover and not to do any talking."

"I'll come to Las Vegas at once," he assured me, "and—"

"And you'll be arrested if you do," I told him. "Minerva's lawyer has got political power here. She picked the best."

"What should I do?" he asked.

"From the way you sound, I think you'd better take a vacation," I told him. "You sound all run down. Evidently you're not accustomed to having the roof fall in on you. You'd better be unavailable for comment."

"And your going to get out, too?"

"Hell, no," I told him, "I'm in the stew. I'm going to stay here and face the music. There's just one chance in a hundred I can salvage something."

"If you can salvage anything, you can write your own ticket," he said. "My Lord, I had no idea anything like this could happen —I suppose *I'm* in it now."

"Your in it now," I told him.

"We'll buy her off," Essex said, after a moment, with a note of hope in his voice. "After all, it's a question of money and with our careers at stake—"

"How much money has your client got?" I asked.

"Plenty."

"And is he willing to give every cent of it to Minerva?"

"Good heavens, it wouldn't be that bad. Even if she could prove infidelity, it—"

"She isn't monkeying with infidelity now," I interrupted. "She's playing with murder."

"Well," said Essex after a moment, "my client has got himself into this. I did the best I could for him. If he gets caught, he's going to have to pay. He gambled, and if he loses, that's a chance he has to take."

"How much money have *you* got?" I asked.

"Me?" he asked. "What's that got to do with it?"

"Don't underestimate Minerva," I said.

"Why . . . why you can't mean—"

"Look up your statutes on murder," I said. "See what the law says about an accessory after the fact."

It took a moment for that to sink in.

"Oh, my God," he said.

I hung up the telephone.

CHAPTER SEVENTEEN

I drove to my hotel and put in a long distance call to Homicide Bureau in Los Angeles. I said it was important that I reach Sergeant Frank Sellers at once with a hot tip. I finally got a night number where I could reach him.

Sellers had evidently been asleep. He was grouchy when he came to the phone.

"Hello, Frank," I said. "This is your friend, Donald."

"Why you . . . you . . . you've got a crust! . . . Friend! Why you pint-sized bastard—"

"Take it easy, Sergeant," I said. "How would you like to talk with Mrs. Harvey W. Chester, the woman who was the victim in that hit-and-run case?"

"What the hell are you trying to do?" he roared into the telephone. "Ringing me up at this hour to give me a razz—"

"She's here in Las Vegas," I said. "If you can get over here right away, I'll put you in touch with her."

"What?"

"You heard me."

"Where are you?"

"Las Vegas."

"And she's there?"

"That's what I said."

"What gives you this sudden change of heart?"

"It isn't a change of heart," I said. "I've always been on the side of law and order, but my motives have been twisted and misinterpreted. I will admit that a couple of smart guys tried to use me. They gave me a double cross but—"

"Where are you?"

I gave him the name of the hotel.

"Wait right there," he said. "If this is a double cross, so help me, I'll beat you to a pulp and throw the pulp into a sausage grinder."

"Have I ever given you a double cross yet?" I asked.

He hesitated a moment. "Well, you've tried damned hard."

"No, I haven't," I said. "I've tried to protect my clients but whenever *I've* given *you* a tip it's been on the up-and-up."

"All right," he said, "I'm going to play along."

"Don't tell anybody about this conversation," I warned. "Just get over here."

After he had hung up, I called Bertha Cool.

Bertha hates night telephone calls.

"Hello, hello, hello," she said testily. "You don't need to ring in my ear just because you got me up out of a sound sleep."

"This is Donald, Bertha," I said. "Grab the first plane for Las Vegas, and I mean the *first* plane. Get over here. I've just finished talking with Frank Sellers. He'll probably get here before you can get a plane, but get here as soon as you can."

"Las Vegas? What the hell are you doing in Las Vegas?"

"Trying to save you embarrassment," I told her. "You'd better get here so you can take charge personally. I think this may call for your technique."

"Well, I'm not coming," she said. "I'm not going to break my neck traipsing around the country trying to pull you out of jams. You went in this on your own. I told you it was your baby and you could change the diapers. Now change them."

"All right," I told her. "It's my baby, but it's sitting in your lap."

"The partnership is dissolved," she said. "You told me that yourself."

Then I told her, "I'll put this fifty thousand fee in my own pocket. Right?"

"What fee?"

"The fifty thousand fee."

"Are you crazy?"

"Not me," I told her.

"Where did you say you were?"

I gave her the name of the hotel.

She hesitated a moment, then grunted, "All right, I'll be there but this had better be good."

"It's going to be good," I told her, "very good indeed."

I hung up the phone, rolled into bed and couldn't sleep.

Sergeant Sellers must have chartered a plane. He was pounding on the door before daylight.

"All right, Pint Size," he said, when I let him in, "what's this about Mrs. Harvey W. Chester?"

"Want to see her?" I asked.

He nodded.

"Okay," I said, "let's go."

I put him in my rented car and we drove down to the drab little bungalow that Mrs. Chester had rented.

We pounded on the door.

For a moment I had a feeling of panic. Then I heard someone moving around on the inside and after a moment the door was opened.

"Hello, Mrs. Chester," I said. "This is Sergeant Sellers of the Los Angeles police force. He's been looking for you."

"Looking for me?" she said, wide-eyed with well-simulated surprise.

"That's right."

"You were involved in a hit-and-run case in Los Angeles," Sellers said.

"Oh," she remarked, looking from Sellers to me.

"We're coming in," Sellers said. "We want to talk with you."

"I'm . . . I'm not dressed."

"You've got a robe on," Sellers said, "that's good enough for us. This isn't a beauty contest. This is investigating a hit-and-run case."

Sellers pushed his way into the apartment. I followed him.

It was the same little two-room apartment with the same drab sitting room, only this time a wall bed had been let down. There was a glimpse of a kitchenette past the bed.

Sellers seated himself in the most comfortable chair in the place. I took a seat on the edge of the bed.

Mrs. Chester stood there looking from one to the other of us.

"All right," Sellers said, "tell me about it."

She said, "I've got to go to the bathroom first."

"Well, make it snappy," Sellers said.

Mrs. Chester went into the bathroom and closed the door.

Sellers looked at me and said, "I'll be damned! I thought you were giving me the runaround."

"It's on the up-and-up," I told him.

"Well, it had better be and don't think for a minute you're going to get any breaks unless you come out of this with a clean nose. You've been cutting too many corners."

I said, "People use me. I tried to find out what it was all about before I told you. That's one thing about me, you know, I never gave you a bum tip. Whenever I tell you anything it pans out."

He took a cigar from his pocket, shoved it into his mouth, said, "I'll reserve judgment on you, Lam."

We sat there waiting. Frank Sellers looked me over.

"You know, Pint Size," he said, "I don't know what kind of a game you're playing but if it's on the up-and-up, I'm going to play along with you."

"Thanks," I said.

"I felt sure you were giving me some kind of a runaround when you telephoned, but one look at that woman's face told me that you were knocking her for a loop. Whatever kind of a deal it is you've cooked up, it isn't a frame-up, not as far as she's concerned," Sellers said. "There's more to this than meets the eye. Those damned cops in Denver claiming that the Eldon car was in Denver the afternoon of the accident—they're all wet! You know and I know that car was involved in an accident."

"Do we?" I asked.

He frowned and said, "Now, don't start pulling that stuff, Pint Size, or I'm going to get mad all over again."

I kept quiet.

He chewed on the cigar for a while.

"There's something fishy about the whole deal," he said after a while.

I said nothing.

"Say," he said, "that dame's been in the bathroom a long time."

He lurched up out of the chair, pounded over to the bathroom door and said, "Come on, make it snappy."

There was no answer.

Sellers looked at me with sudden consternation. "Hell, she couldn't get out of the bathroom window dressed like that," he said.

The sound of a toilet flushing came through the door.

Sellers grunted, went back and sat down.

There was more silence.

Finally Sellers got up and went over to the bathroom door again. "Come on out," he said.

She said, "I can't come out."

"Come on out," he told her, "you've been in there long enough. Let's go."

"I'm not ready."

Sellers banged on the door. "Open it up."

"I tell you I can't."

Sellers' face flushed. "Say, what kind of gag is this?" he said. "Get the hell out of there. Open up."

"Just a minute," she said sweetly, "I'll be there. Don't hurry me too much."

Sellers came back and sat down. He scowled at me.

I said, "She must have been in there ten minutes."

"Well," Sellers said.

I shrugged my shoulders.

We waited another minute or two.

"What does a cop do," I asked, "when someone gives him a runaround by sitting in a bathroom?"

"I'll show you what a cop does," Sellers said, savagely. He got out of the chair, walked over to the bathroom door, said, "Open up."

"Just a few minutes now,"

"Open up," Sellers said.

"I'm not ready to open up."

"Open that door," Sellers said, "or I'll kick it in."

"You wouldn't *dare* do that," she said. "I have a right to go to the bathroom. I—"

Sellers stepped back, stood on his left foot, elevated his right foot and lashed out with a flatfooted impact, hitting the door just back of the doorknob.

The door shivered.

"Come on," Sellers said, "I'll bust it down."

"I told you I can't come out now."

Seller cocked his right foot and gave another terrific blow.

The door shivered. There was a sound of splintering wood. The door slammed open, hit against a doorstop and vibrated.

Mrs. Chester was standing there with her robe around her, looking out of an open window. It was about eight feet to the ground.

"None of that," Sellers said.

"How dare you!" she said. "How dare you break in on me this way.

"You've been in here fifteen minutes already," Sellers said, "that's time enough to clean your teeth, brush your hair, powder your nose, take a shower and do everything else you needed to do ten times over. I don't want a runaround, I want the truth. Now come out here."

She gave one last look at the open window, then marched out.

Sellers dropped back into his seat, indicated a straightback chair for her. "Sit down there," he said. "Lam, you sit on the bed."

Sellers turned to her, wolfed the cigar around in his mouth, said, "what about this hit-and-run business?"

"What hit-and-run?"

Sellers said, "You complained of a hit-and-run incident."

"It was stupid of me," she said.

Sellers frowned.

"Actually it was mostly my fault," she said. "I turned around and wanted to see something and kept right on walking, and I walked right into this car."

"You were in a pedestrian crossing?"

"Yes."

"And the car was coming how fast?"

"I don't know," she said. "I'm beginning to think the car was standing still."

"What?" Sellers yelled.

She nodded and said to me, "I'm sorry I took advantage of you, Donald, because you're a nice boy, but after all this is a cruel world. A person has to look out for number one."

"What do you mean the car was standing still?" Sellers asked.

"I didn't say it was. I said it *might* have been for all I know."

"That isn't the way you told it to the police," Sellers said.

"The police never gave me a chance. They acted on the assumption that the car was moving just because I was hit on a pedestrian zone."

"You were hit?"

"Well *I* may have hit the car, I don't know. I was walking along and all of a sudden there was this impact on my shoulder and I went down and the next thing I knew people were running all around me and somebody shouted, 'Get an ambulance,' and—"

"And what happened to the car?"

"The car went away."

"Then it was a hit-and-run," Sellers said.

"Well," she said thoughtfully, "it was a run, I guess."

I said, "Did you give the driver of the car your name and address?"

"No, why?"

"But you went away in an ambulance?"

"Yes."

"Did you need to?"

She smiled archly and said, "Now, I was afraid you were going to ask that question, Donald, and I'm just not going to answer it. After all, I'm a helpless, lone widow and I have to look out for myself."

Sellers grunted.

"Now," Mrs. Chester went on, "that's the peculiar thing about the law. The law says that if a motorist hits a pedestrian he has to stop and give aid, but it doesn't say anything about a pedestrian

100

hitting a motorist having to stop and give aid. At least I don't think it does."

"You've looked up the law?" I asked.

"It's been looked up," she said.

"You let Donald Lam here make a settlement of ten thousand bucks on you?" Sellers asked.

"Now," she said, "it wasn't that way at all. Donald Lam will tell you the true facts."

"I want *you* to tell me the true facts."

"Well, Donald Lam called on me. At first he said he was selling magazines. Then I told him about the accident and he said he knew a person who sometimes bought up accident claims for cash and then filed suit and got a lot more money. I let him know that I would be interested."

"You mean he'd pay you money and suit would never be filed," Sellers said.

"Heavens to Betsy," she said, "it was nothing like that at all. He was buying the claim because he wanted to make more money out of it."

Sellers quit looking at her and started looking at me. "You know, Pint Size," he said, thoughtfully, "I'm beginning to smell something here, and I hope your hands are clean."

"This is all news to me," I said, "except that she's telling the truth about the fact that I told her I wasn't representing an insurance company and wasn't making any settlement; that I knew a person who sometimes bought claims and then recovered on them."

Sellers glowered at me. "Played it pretty smart, didn't you?"

"The way she talked," I said, "she had a very good claim if a person could find the car that hit her."

"I see," Sellers said, "and by a rare coincidence the person that you went to get the money from was the person who was driving the car that hit her."

There was the banging of peremptory knuckles on the door and a man's voice said, "Open up in here."

Mrs. Chester jumped up with alacrity and opened the door.

A man of about fifty, with broad shoulders, a bull neck, a florid red face and feverish little brown eyes, set wide apart over a jaw that would have graced a prize fighter, said, "What the hell's going on here?"

Sellers got up to face him, pushed the cigar out and upward at an aggressive angle. "And may I ask who the hell you are?"

The man said, "I'm Marvin Estep Fowler. I'm an attorney at

law. I'm representing Mrs. Chester here, and I want to know what's going on. Now, who are you?"

Sellers said, "I'm Sergeant Sellers." He pulled a leather container out of his pocket and flashed a badge at Fowler.

"Just a minute, just a minute," Fowler said, as Sellers started to put the leather folder back in his pocket.

Fowler took the folder, looked at the badge and said, "Uh-huh, Los Angeles, huh?"

"That's right," Sellers said.

"I didn't know the city limits of Los Angeles stretched into Nevada," Fowler said.

"They don't."

"Then you're out of your jurisdiction," Fowler said.

"I'm working on a lead on a case—a hot lead."

"And the way to do that," Fowler said, "is to check in at police headquarters here, get a local man on the job and the two of you work on it together with the local man taking the responsibility."

"There wasn't time for all that," Sellers said, but the angle of his cigar dropped three degrees.

The lawyer whirled to me. "And who are you?"

"The name's Lam," I said. "Donald Lam."

Mrs. Chester said, "He's the one I was telling you about late last night, Mr. Fowler. He's the man that gave me the money and had me execute an assignment of my damage claim against anyone that hit me—or," she added with a smile, "that I might have hit, only I didn't tell him that."

Fowler said to Mrs. Chester, "Your note said you were waiting in the bathroom."

"He kicked the door down," she said, pointing to Sellers.

"He what?" Fowler asked.

"Kicked the door down."

"Show me."

She led him over to the bathroom and showed him the splintered wood.

"Well, I'll be damned," Fowler said.

"Let's see if I get the sketch," Sellers said to Mrs. Chester. "You went to the bathroom, opened the window and threw out a note. Is that right?"

She beamed and smiled. "That's right. I wanted my attorney. I thought I had a right to have him here so I threw out a note to an awfully nice little girl who read it and smiled at me and nodded her head to show that she understood. She went to a telephone and called this number Mr. Fowler had left with me."

Sellers' face got black. He looked from her to Fowler, then from Fowler to me.

"Where do you fit into this, Pint Size?" he asked.

"I told you where I fitted in it. I was giving you the information you wanted. All this other stuff is news to me. You're the one who let her go to the bathroom and lock the door."

"You got any charge against my client?" Fowler asked Sellers. "—In Los Angeles, that is."

"I don't know," Sellers said thoughtfully. He suddenly whirled to Mrs. Chester and said, "Have you ever been in other hit-and-run cases?"

"Well," she said thoughtfully, "I—"

"Don't answer that," Fowler interposed. "You don't have to."

Sellers was frowning and chewing on his cigar. "It seems to me I am beginning to remember some things," he said.

Sellers was frowningly contemplative for a minute. Suddenly he whirled to Mrs. Chester, said, "What's your name?"

"Mrs. Harvey W. Chester," she said.

"That's your husband's name. You're a widow."

"Yes."

"Your first name is Tessie—T-E-S-S-I-E?" he asked, abruptly. She said, with dignity, "My first name is Theresa."

A slow grin spread over Seller's face. "I get you now," he said. "Tessie—*Tessie the Tumbler*, that's your speciality, doing a flip-flop on the pedestrian crossing and then claiming you've been involved in a hit-and-run."

Sellers turned to me. He was grinning. "Looks like you got taken, Pint Size," he said. "You fell for the good old tumbling trick—Now, wait a minute . . . wait a minute."

Sellers got to his feet, stood with his legs apart, his face thrust forward, chewing on the cigar. The grin remained on his features. "Now," he said "we're beginning to get to the real core of the apple. And isn't that pretty! I'm going to tell you something, Pint Size, maybe you're just a sucker on this thing, maybe you're the mastermind, but whoever is the mastermind is going to get into lots and lots and lots of trouble."

"And," Fowler said, "just so *you* don't get into lots of trouble yourself, Sergeant, I think it would be advisable for you to get out of here, check in at the police station and ask for official courtesies in the official manner."

Sellers turned savagely to him. "Any time I want anything out of your bailiwick I'll ask for it," he said. "Right now I'm on my own."

He strode over to the telephone, picked it up, dialed information, said, "I want the airport. This is Sergeant Sellers of police, just connect me with the airport."

A moment later, he asked, "When is your next plane to Denver?"

He frowned and looked at his watch. "Not until then?"

He hesitated a moment, then said, "All right, get me a seat on it. Sergeant Sellers, Los Angeles Police Department."

Sellers banged up the telephone, turned to Fowler and said, "I'll be talking with you later."

He turned to me. "If you actually paid ten thousand bucks in cash," he said, "it probably lets you out. But if you just paid ten grand in conversation it means you were masterminding the whole thing."

"I paid ten grand in cash," I said.

"Let's hope so for Bertha's sake," he said, and walked out.

Fowler held the door open for me, "And I see no need to detain you any further, Mr. Lam."

I walked out. It was Minerva's trick all the way.

CHAPTER EIGHTEEN

I drove the rented car up to the motel I'd rented, unlocked the door and went in.

I looked at the door leading to Elsie Brand's room. It was tightly closed.

I went to the bathroom, gave my hands and face a good scrubbing with a hot washcloth, and came out feeling a little better.

Things were whirling around now like an electric fan. But that's better than having them get static in an unfavorable position. While things are moving around, it's always possible to reach in and grab out something that you want. When they freeze in an unfavorable position, you're frozen, too.

I walked over toward the connecting door intending to knock, when there was the sound of a gentle, almost surreptitious knock at the outer door of my cabin.

I hesitated a moment.

The knock was repeated.

I went to the door, opened it a crack.

Minerva Badger was there.

"Hello, Donald," she said.

Her voice was dripping with syrup.

"Hello to you," I said.

I thought I heard a motion behind me.

"May I come in, Donald?"

"Who's with you?"

"I'm all alone."

"Where's this lawyer of yours?"

"Oh, you've met him?"

"You know I have."

"He's in his office, I guess."

"How are the trump cards?" I asked. "Still got every one in the deck?"

"Donald, I have to talk with you about that."

"Go on and talk."

"Not here."

"Come on in," I invited.

She came into the room.

"You act pretty fast," she said.

"Do I?"

"You just take the bit in your teeth and start going. You don't give a person a chance to talk with you."

"You're talking now."

"I need you, Donald."

"*You* do?"

"Yes."

"I thought you had every trump in the deck."

"That's the trouble," she said. "I think I have every trump in the deck, but I don't know what's trumps. I think you do."

"Talk some more," I invited.

She said, "You know who I am, don't you?"

"Yes."

"Did you know who I was when I got on the plane?"

"I suspected it."

"How? What tipped you off?"

"Your clothes, your manner, the fact that you had followed me aboard the plane and then dropped into the seat beside me, the approach, the whole thing."

"What about my clothes?"

"You were too well groomed for a detective or any kind of a woman having a job; you radiated money."

"I took my big diamond off," she said.

"I know you did," I told her, "and the indentation in the flesh of the finger was very obvious."

"All right," she said, "you had me spotted and you've got me spotted now. But I need you."

"How?"

"You had a job to do. You did it. You can help me now."

"In what way?"

"My Denver lawyer has negotiated a property settlement. It's not a very good property settlement. If I had the proof that my husband had been playing around and I could put my finger on the girl he'd been playing around with, I could make a lot more money."

"How much more?"

"A whole lot more."

"So what do you want me to do?"

"Talk."

"I can't tell you anything that will help you."

"Can't or won't?"

"Can't."

"You mean because you don't know, or because of professional ethics?"

"I mean I can't tell you a thing that will help you."

She came over close to me, put her hands on my shoulders. "Look, Donald, I admit that I played tag with you on the plane. I wanted to talk with you. I thought perhaps a little sex would win you over and bring you into my camp.

"Now then, you've avoided me and left me in a spot where I hold a whole fistful of cards that I think are trumps, but I can't establish that they are trumps without your help.

"You're young. You're working for money. You could have *lots* of money."

I shook my head.

"And," she said seductively, "you could go places—the Italian Riviera, the Alps, round-the-world cruises, and you could have—you could have your choice of women."

She was standing close to me now. "You know what I mean, Donald? Your choice."

"Wouldn't that be rather hard to explain?" I asked.

"Phooey on explanations," she said. "We'd make a settlement. I'd get a divorce, and you and I could be on a boat within forty-eight hours. We could go anywhere you wanted—do anything you wanted—anything.

"Donald, please, please."

Her arms were around my neck now. "You can't be just a thinking machine. You have to be a human, Donald, and I'm human, too, and from the minute I saw you I liked you—fell for you.

"I want—"

The sound which came from the closet was a combination of a suppressed sneeze and a strangled cough. It sounded like a thunderclap.

Minerva Badger jumped away from me as though I'd suddenly turned red hot. She gained the door to the closet in four swift strides and jerked it open.

Elsie Brand was seated there holding a handkerchief to her mouth, her eyes wide and glassy, the tape recorder running, the shorthand book in her lap filled with pothooks.

"And what, may I ask, is the meaning of this?" Minerva Badger demanded.

I had time only to flash Elsie one quick wink. "My God," I said, *"my wife!"*

"Your *wife!*" Minerva shouted.

"Good heavens, Elsie," I said, "how in the world did *you* get here and how long have you been here?"

Again I handed her a wink.

Elsie did her best to carry off the part. She got to her feet and said indignantly, "Long enough. I'd heard you were carrying on with a rich divorcee in Las Vegas."

She reached over, put the tape recorder into highspeed reverse, rewound the tape, picked the spool off the spindle, put it in her purse, picked up her shorthand book, tucked her chin in the air, marched right through the apartment and out the front door.

Minerva stood looking at me with consternation all over her face. "You never told me you were married," she said.

"You didn't ask me," I told her, "*You* were the fortuneteller. *You* were looking in *my* hand. Couldn't you tell?"

"Don't crack smart with me, Donald Lam. I didn't know you were married."

I shrugged my shoulders.

"What's she going to do with that tape recording?" she asked.

"Probably sue me for divorce and name you as co-respondent."

"I didn't do anything," she said.

"It depends on what's on that tape recorder and what Elsie says about the tone of your voice. It probably sounded rather seductive to a jealous wife sitting in a closet listening—getting evidence for divorce case."

"Good Lord," Minerva said, "of all the damned messes."

She walked over to the telephone, dialed a number and said into the telephone, "Marvin . . . I guess you'd better get down here to this motel I told you about. I seem to have walked into a trap of some kind."

She looked up from the instrument to glower at me and said, "At least I'm beginning to think it was a trap—No," she said into the telephone, "I want *you* to come down *here*—that's right—right away."

She hung up the telephone.

She looked at me and said, "All right, your wife is gone, the tape recorder is gone. I'll put it on the line. There's evidence that exists that my husband was unfaithful. I want that evidence."

"How do you know it exists?"

"I . . . I *know.*"

"What kind of evidence?"

"I believe there's tangible evidence."

Peremptory knuckles sounded in a preliminary knock on the door and then the door was shoved open.

Frank Sellers stood on the threshold. "All right, Pint Size," he said, "let's go."

"Where?"

"Los Angeles. . . . Who's the dame?"

"Mrs. Badger," I said, "may I present my warm, personal friend, Sergeant Frank Sellers of the Los Angeles police."

She froze up. "Indeed," she said, then nodded very distantly. "Good morning, Sergeant Sellers."

Sellers looked her over, said, "I'd like to talk with you, Mrs. Badger."

"Her attorney is on his way down here," I said. "I think you've met the attorney. His name is Fowler. I believe it's Marvin Estep Fowler."

Sellers made some remark under his breath.

Minerva Badger stood looking at Sellers, apparently unable to take her eyes off him.

Sellers said, "Come on, Pint Size, we're leaving quick."

"How?"

"Charter plane, a fast one."

"Where?" I asked. "To Denver?"

He shook his head. "Los Angeles." He shifted the cigar in his mouth and said, "I'm going to get to the bottom of this if it takes the whole police force to do it. There's something fishy about this and I don't like it. This Tessie the Tumbler may be sitting pretty with an attorney to represent her in Las Vegas, but unless she gives me the information I want, she's going to be extradited to California to face a couple of criminal conspiracy warrants there, and I think I'm going to have the goods on her."

I looked at Minerva. There was, for a moment, sheer panic in her eyes, then she looked desperately at her wrist watch.

I did some thinking, said to Sellers, "Want to wait until after the attorney gets here, or go now?"

"We go now," Sellers said. "Do you get it? *Now.*"

We went.

I had thought Sellers was planning to give me a third degree on the plane, but he sat there chewing on his cigar saying nothing.

"What's the idea?" I asked, when we looked down at the Los Angeles airport.

"I'm getting back in my own bailiwick," he said. "Denver can come to me and Las Vegas can come to me. I don't need to go to them."

"What do you want?"

"I don't know yet, Pint Size," he said. "I know that I want you, but I don't know just how I'm going to get at you right now. Maybe you're a friend. That is, maybe you want to act friendly. If you do, I'll give you a break. Maybe you want to play smart aleck. If you do, it's going to be too bad. And," he added, taking the cigar from his mouth and poking the end at me in little forceful gestures, "maybe you tried to mastermind this whole damned business, and if you did it's going to be just awfully too bad. You're going to lose a lot more than your license. You're going to lose your liberty."

"And what do I do now, consider myself in custody?"

"I want to know where you are every five minutes," Sellers said. "Go on to your apartment. Go to your office. Go see your best girl. Have a good dinner, go to bed if you want to, but be where I can put my hand on you at five minutes' notice. And if you think I'm kidding, just try to duck out and see what happens. I'll have you where I can put my hand on you any time, day or night."

I said, "Okay, I'll be at my apartment," and went home.

I called the Las Vegas motel and asked for Elsie. She had checked out. I called Las Vegas and asked for Minerva Badger. Her phone didn't answer. I called Denver, Colorado, and tried to get Alting Badger. I was advised he was unavailable.

I said that I would talk with Mellie Belden.

After a moment, her voice came on the line—cool, calm, competent, "May I take a message?" she asked. "This is Mr. Badger's secretary."

"You may take a message," I said. "Tell Badger not to get panic-stricken, to sit tight and continue to be unavailable."

"I take it this is Mr. Lam talking?"

"That's right."

"He's told me about you," she said. "Thank you. I'll see that the message is delivered—if it's at all possible."

I took a bath, thought some of ringing the office, decided against it, rang up the airport, asked about Las Vegas schedules, found that there were several planes which had left shortly after I had left with Sellers in his chartered plane.

I rang Elsie Brand's apartment.

No answer.

I put on clean clothes, mixed myself a drink, waited.

A gentle knock sounded on the door.

I opened it.

Elsie Brand was on the threshold.

"Oh, Donald," she asked, "Donald, are you all right?"

"So far," I told her, "I'm all right."

She came rushing into the apartment and threw her arms around me. "Donald, I'm so glad, so terribly, terribly glad. I was afraid that you'd be . . . well, in trouble."

"I am in trouble."

She laughed and said, "I meant in jail."

"I'm not in jail," I said, and then added significantly, "yet."

"Oh, Donald, you—"

The door which had been left ajar was pushed open, and Minerva Badger stood on the threshold.

She looked at Elsie and said, "I was on the same plane with you, Mrs. Lam, but you didn't know it. You were in tourist. I was in the first class section."

She seated herself and said, "All right, what are we going to do about it—but I want to assure you of this much, Mrs. Lam, I had no idea that Donald was married."

I slipped an arm around Elsie's waist and said, "I think Elsie is forgiving me, but that doesn't necessarily mean she's forgiving you. You tried to buy me with sex."

"With sex and money," Minerva Badger said. "Those are the two things I happen to have the most of at the moment."

I drew Elsie close to me, "Don't mind her, honey," I said. "She's being a little coarse. I never did fall for her."

"All right," Minerva went on, "so now we find out the guy is married. It's okay with me. We'll leave the sex out of it and start talking money."

"How much money?" I asked, holding Elsie in my arms so that Minerva couldn't see her face.

"Lot's of money," she said, "provided I get what I want."

"And what do you want?"

"Let's not mince words. A nasty little blackmailer named Deering Canby had evidence, lots of evidence. He unfortunately died very suddenly and no one has been able to find the evidence."

"No one?" I asked.

"No one," she said firmly. "I retained a Denver attorney and Mr. Canby's apartment was searched, ostensibly to look for a will, but my attorney had permission from Canby's heirs to go through the apartment with a fine-tooth comb. He did it. There wasn't a smell of what we wanted. However, there was enough stuff to show that Canby was a professional blackmailer. . . . Now then, that opens up interesting possibilities."

"Are you sure he had the stuff you wanted, this man, Canby?"
I asked.

"Of course I'm sure."

The door was suddenly pushed open. Sergeant Frank Sellers, accompanied by Bertha Cool, barged into the room.

"Well, I'll be damned," Sellers said. "We've got in on a family party."

"Elsie," Bertha screamed. "What are *you* doing here?"

Elsie broke away from my arm hastily, with flaming cheeks.

"You didn't show up at the office," Bertha said. "I should have known that you were lolligagging around with Donald somewhere. Sending *me* on wild-goose chases to Nevada!"

Minerva's face showed a whole series of expressions.

"Who's the Jane?" Bertha asked.

"Minerva Badger," I said. "Las Vegas for the purpose of establishing a six weeks' residence. More recently of Denver, Colorado."

Sellers said, "All right, Pint Size, I've got Bertha Cool with me now and this is it. This is the showdown. Put your cards right out on the table."

I said, "Okay, I will."

"Not until I've put some of mine on the table," Minerva Badger said bitterly. "You want evidence that will send this guy to jail and I've got it. And for your information I can be had. All I need is a little co-operation."

Sellers looked at her with interest.

"And for your information," I said to Sellers, "this woman murdered Deering L. Canby."

"What?" Sellers exclaimed.

I said, "Canby had some evidence that he wanted to peddle to the highest bidder. He gave Badger the first crack at it. He told him not to be over two minutes late. That meant that he must have had a second appointment provided he and Badger couldn't come to terms.

"The second appointment was with Minerva Badger here."

"She kept her appointment. She found him groggy, apparently about half drunk. It was a swell opportunity for her to get what she wanted without paying a red dime. She carries a little phial of chloral hydrate in her purse—at one time she was a nurse.

"She fed the guy knockout drops.

"Things had been happening she didn't know about. The knockout drops were cumulative. He fell over dead. She searched him carefully, couldn't find the evidence she wanted, couldn't even find the keys to his apartment. She was baffled. She slipped out of the picture back to Las Vegas and consulted with her attorney."

There was a sudden, heavy pounding of knuckles on the door, then almost immediately the knob turned, the door opened and Marvin Estep Fowler stood on the threshold. "I got here as soon as I could, Minerva," he said. "I . . ." He broke off as he saw the number of people in the room and the tense, strained attitudes.

"And what are you doing here?" Sellers asked Fowler.

"I'm here representing my client, Mrs. Alting L. Badger. And I'd like to know what this is all about."

"What do you mean you're representing her?" Sellers asked.

"I'm representing her as an attorney."

"The hell you are," Sellers said. "You're an attorney in Nevada. I didn't know that the Nevada state line ran into the city of Los Angeles. You ever been admitted to practice law in California?"

"I can advise my client."

"Just go ahead," Sellers said, "and I'll pinch you for practicing law without a license, impersonating an officer of the court and violating the Business and Professional Code."

I took advantage of the strained silence and said, "Canby was a blackmailer. He had information that he wanted to sell. You know what he had in his mind as well as I do. He was selling it to the highest bidder. He had Badger come first; his wife was to come second. Canby was too smart to have the stuff in his possession, but Minerva here thought he had it in his possession. She slipped him the chloral hydrate and—"

"I'm going to sue you for slander and defamation of character," Fowler said.

I said to Sellers, "She's got a little bottle of chloral hydrate in her purse right now. She was planning to slip me a Mickey Finn if she couldn't do business with me."

Sellers reached for the purse.

"Don't you touch that purse," Fowler warned, pointing a finger at him. "You have no reasonable grounds for search. All you have is the slanderous, defamatory statement of this young man here."

Sellers hesitated.

I said, "Do you have any objection if we look in your purse, Mrs. Badger?"

"I most certainly do," she said. "In fact, I'm going to get out of here."

"Not until I've had a chance to question you," Sellers said.

He turned to Fowler. "But you can go. You're not doing any good here. You can't do any good. You can't practice law in California. You're out of your territory. As you so aptly pointed out to me, the logical thing would have been to have stopped in, explained the circumstances to some resident Los Angeles attorney and had him accompany you."

"Don't tell me how to practice law."

"I'm telling you how I'll practice law," Sellers said. "Get out!"

"What do you mean?"

"Just two words," Sellers said, advancing belligerently, "get out!"

"My client sent for me."

"I'll make it one word," Sellers said. "*Out.*"

Fowler backed toward the door, "Now look," he said, "you can't do this, you can't—"

"The hell I can't," Sellers said. He turned to me, "You want him out, Pint Size?—It's your apartment."

I nodded.

Sellers opened the door with his left hand, bunched a fistful of Fowler's shirt and necktie in his right hand and heaved.

Fowler went out of the door backwards so fast he slammed against the wall on the other side of the hall.

Sellers kicked the door shut and dusted his hands. "I'd like to look in your purse," he said to Minerva.

"You can go straight to hell," she said. "I'm going out."

"Remember," I told her, "Elsie has a tape recording of your conversation and—"

"You rat," she said, and swung her hand with the purse as hard as she could swing it.

A rough spot in the catch scratched down the side of my cheek and drew blood.

I said to Sellers, "Arrest her."

"What for?" Sellers asked.

"Assault and battery," I said. "Actually I think that purse is a deadly weapon."

"You going to prosecute?" he asked.

"It gives you a good excuse to take her to headquarters," I said, "and once you've got her down there you have to remove all personal property from her purse and give her a receipt."

A slow smile spread over Seller's features.

She took one look at him, then whirled and said, "Don't you dare put your hands on me, you big brute."

"Deputize *me*, Frank," Bertha said.

"You're deputized," Sellers said.

Bertha reached out one long, meaty arm as heavy as the average leg, clamped it around the back of Minerva Badger's dress and slammed her across the room.

Bertha came waddling after her like a Japanese wrestler, head forward, arms out.

Minerva swung the purse again. Bertha blocked it. The catch came open. The contents were strewn all over the rug.

Bertha threw her arms around Minerva, pinioned her by expertly twisting her wrists around behind her back. "Got any handcuffs, Frank?" she asked.

Sellers hesitated a moment.

"I'm a deputy," Bertha said. "She resisted arrest. Isn't it a crime to resist an officer in the performance of his duties?"

Sellers gave her the handcuffs.

I was down on my hands and knees looking around on the rug.

"Here it is," I said, pointing to a small vial. "Chloral hydrate, otherwise known as knockout drops."

Bertha slammed Minerva down into a chair. "Wait there for the paddy wagon," she said.

"You're hurting!" Minerva screamed. "Those handcuffs are breaking the bones in my wrists."

"Quit trying to jerk loose," Bertha said. "That makes them bite all the deeper. Sit there and shut up."

Sellers looked at me. "This man, Canby, was killed by a dose of chloral hydrate?"

"That's what the autopsy surgeon says."

A slow grin spread over Sellers' countenance. "I guess it isn't going to hurt anything if the California cops solve a Colorado killing."

"Now listen," Minerva said, "let's talk sense. You're talking about murder. I didn't give him enough to hurt him. All I gave him was a dose that would knock him out for about an hour. You can't pin a murder rap on that."

"Perhaps not," I said, "but we can sure pin a manslaughter rap. And that isn't going to help your divorce case any."

Sellers had been doing a lot of thinking. He nodded to Bertha. "You're still a deputy," he said. "Get her up out of there; let's go before some smart lawyer gets a writ."

115

CHAPTER NINETEEN

Headlines in the paper said:

DENVER SOCIALITE CONFESSES ACCIDENTAL KILLING OF BLACKMAILER

Los Angeles Police Score Signal Triumph in Cleaning up Colorado Killing

The article went on to state that in an investigation of the death of a blackmailer, well-meaning witnesses in Colorado had thrown the police off the track by giving them the license number of a car which had later proved to have been out of the state at the time; that a character known as Tessie the Tumbler had, by a stroke of luck, picked that car for one of her fraudulent tumbling acts by which she had in the past victimized insurance companies.

In this instance it seemed that the driver of the car had preferred to make an out-of-court settlement, but under the circumstances felt no desire to prosecute "Tumbling Tess," as she was known to the police, for obtaining money by false pretenses.

The newspaper even mentioned that Frank Sellers had modestly admitted that a local firm of private detectives, Cool and Lam, had been of considerable assistance to him in clearing up the case.

The Colorado police were investigating the death of the blackmailer but it was doubtful if they would prosecute the wealthy socialite as police felt the death had been due to a "combination of circumstances."

The woman's husband, one of Denver's leading and influential businessmen, had interceded on her behalf. While the couple were in the process of getting a divorce, an amicable property settlement had been worked out and there was even talk of a reconciliation.

In any event the Denver police, glad to have a puzzling death straightened out, had uncovered evidence linking the dead man to a whole series of nefarious blackmail plots.

Elsie was looking over my shoulder as we read the paper, hot off the press.

CUT THIN TO WIN

Her arms came around my neck. "Donald," she breathed, "you're *wonderful!*"

The phone rang.

Elsie picked up the instrument, said, "Mr. Lam's office.... He's busy now. . . . Just a moment."

She turned to me. "Colton C. Essex," she said.

I reached for the instrument. "Hello, Essex," I said.

"Seen the papers?" he asked.

"Just reading them."

"Everything under control?"

"Perfectly safe. I see the Badgers may become reconciled."

"That's right."

"Where will that leave the other woman in the case?"

"She's okay. She got a nice chunk of money for co-operating. She knows she can't win 'em all. Anyhow, I'm keeping my eye on her—you know what I mean, looking out for her interests."

"Yes," I said, "I know what you mean."

There was a moment's silence. "You had Badger well hidden?" I asked.

Essex said, "Hell, he was in Mexico City within five hours of the time they picked you up in Colorado. What kind of a lawyer do you think I am?"

"A pretty good one," I said, "provided you remember your comment that we weren't working for peanuts."

He said, "That's one of the things I wanted to talk to you about.

"I think Mrs. Badger may be able to beat the rap in Colorado, but she's going to need her husband's influence, and no more evidence against her than is, what you might say, readily available.

"Mr. Badger feels that you need a good, long vacation where you won't be interrupted by telephone calls or people who want to talk to you about this case. I've been instructed to put a fifty-thousand-dollar deposit into your account covering your services to date and giving you an opportunity to take a good, long vacation. You will, of course, want to have your secretary with you."

"Where we can't be questioned by the Colorado police?" I asked.

"I didn't say that," he said, hastily. "*You* said that."

"Thanks a lot," I told him.

"You should start on that vacation immediately."

"I never was one to dillydally with a vacation," I said, "but I can't just leave all my business."

"We didn't expect you to," he said. "Your secretary can handle

117

matters which come up while you're in Acapulco. Take her along. Be *sure* to take her."

I hung up the telephone.

Elsie had been monitoring the conversation on the other phone. Her eyes were wide. "Fifty—thousand—dollars," she said. "Good heavens, what will Bertha say when she hears about all these developments?"

I said, "I know exactly what she'll say. She'll say, 'Fry me for an oyster. I never could understand this goddam sex stuff. Here we get this client out of a jam with his wife, and then he goes and gets all tangled up again. Sex doesn't make sense.'

"That's what Bertha will say, but right now you start looking up planes to Mexico City and Acapulco. We'll go to Tijuana and embark from there."

"Donald, do I . . . that is, am I really supposed—"

"You heard what the lawyer said," I told her.

"It will take me a while to pack and—Oh, Donald, I feel terribly self-conscious!"

"No packing," I said. "We go down to the parking lot, get in the car and head for Tijuana, just like that.

"We'll let Essex break the news to Bertha after we're safely out of the country. This is business. We have to see a client."

>>> If you've enjoyed this book and would like to discover more great vintage crime and thriller titles, as well as the most exciting crime and thriller authors writing today, visit: >>>

The Murder Room
Where Criminal Minds Meet

themurderroom.com

www.ingramcontent.com/pod-product-compliance
Ingram Content Group UK Ltd.
Pitfield, Milton Keynes, MK11 3LW, UK
UKHW022308280225
455674UK00004B/217

9 781471 909221